Mystery in the Bowels of the Earth

A NOVEL

BY

Yossi Soika

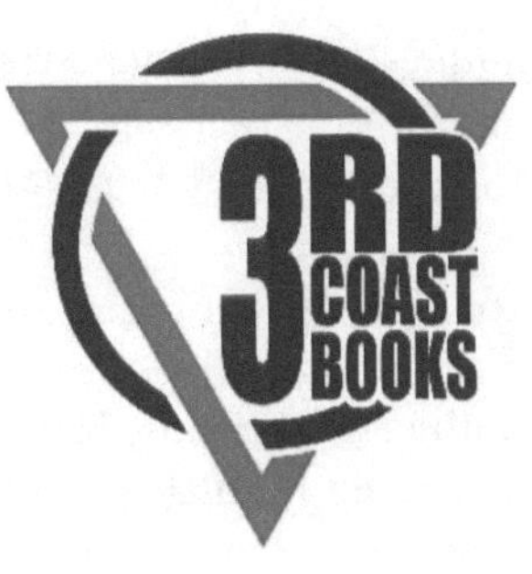

3rd Coast Books, LLC
19790 Hwy. 105 W. Ste. 1318
Montgomery, Texas 77356

3rd Coast Books, LLC
19790 Hwy. 105 W. Ste. 1318
Montgomery, TX 77356

www.3rd CoastBooks.com

ISBNs
Perfect Binding (Print) 978-1-946743-33-6
eBook/Mobi 978-1-946743-34-3
eBook/ePub 978-1-946743-35-0

Project Coordinator - Ian W. Gorman, Associate Publisher
Editor - Ian W. Gorman
Cover Artist - Kathleen J. Shields, Kathleen's Graphics
Text Designer - Kathleen J. Shields, Kathleen's Graphics
Translator - Naama Miron Asher

Printed in the United States of America

READER TESTIMONIALS

"Unique, interesting, and fascinating! That is how I would describe Yossi's "Mystery in The Bowels of The Earth". Moreover, Yossi tells a sweet yet adventure-filled story about a young couple exploring Israel."
— **Kimberly Edwards**

"Mystery in the Bowels of the Earth for me is a story of perseverance, hope, and what could almost be deemed a miracle is so moving and so inspiring you will feel like cheering at the end. Truly cathartic." — **Terrance Castillo**

"Is it a real documented story or a daydream? Was the author telling us about his version of reality or is this just merely for entertainment? Those are some of the things I thought about while I was reading this book! The book is quite imaginative and some points are actually recorded facts in History too!" — **Barbara Hernandez**

"Filled with adventure, mystery, and humor! I really like the dynamics of this piece by Yossi! I am also greatly impressed by his ideas and concepts. What's more is that, apart from being entertained and immersed, you will become highly knowledgeable! You will learn about Judaism, Jewish culture, and tradition. Furthermore, you will also be able to test your own theories about God and the human mind. It is indeed a POWERFUL BOOK!" — **Marsha James**

"If you ever wanted to use the words Epic and Brilliant in a book review, Mystery in the Bowels of the Earth is a book that upholds that accolade. It is a fabulous masterpiece of historical fiction, based in Israel hundreds of years ago. The sense of time and place are vividly drawn and the fragility of life shadow each of the characters." — **Elijah Adams**

DEDICATION

I dedicate this book to my partner for the last 10 years Nava. She excels in many ways and through the many things she does.

CONTENTS

PREFACE

This book is based upon a strange series of events that happened to me, what now seems to be, a very long time ago. So, why am I telling this story today? I really don't know where to begin. Let's just say that this story is so unusual, you probably won't believe it. You'll possibly think that I am fantasizing, confusing dreams with reality ... and maybe I am. Have a read and see where my story takes you.

— Yossi Soika

When I was young I loved to read adventure books. Somehow, as a child, these adventures were seen as a promise — that the world has unity in it of excitement and wakefulness. I grew up to work with all kinds of texts. I believe that the adventures of Dan and Sue in Yossi Soika's book bring us back to such an exciting and awakening promise.

— Naama Miron Asher

Translator from the original Hebrew

The world will build grace;

A land without grace will not reap a harvest.

Chapter 1

The Promise

First, let me introduce myself. My name is Dan. I live in a small town called Larchmont in New York State. I like candy, interesting books, and clever girls. I hate harsh winter days, boring teachers, and evil, arrogant people. My story begins on the 23rd of April 1968, which was my sixteenth birthday. Late April days in Larchmont are wonderful. The snow melts slowly and the trees open their first buds of new life, releasing intoxicating scents into the air. The scents make me feel more alive, reminding me that the cold, snowy winter is about to disappear and that I can now enjoy spending more time outdoors.

On that day I went with my father to the nearby town of Mamaroneck, where we bought some things that we needed for our trip to Israel. My father works at a large commercial company searching for new energy sources to replace our rapidly diminishing oil reserves. Dad is an expert on solar energy, and in Israel, the Weizmann Institute of Science was about to host a very important conference in this area. This is why my father was going to Israel. You are probably wondering why I was going with him … well, it was thanks to my academic achievements in high-school. "If you achieve a high average on your report card, I will take you on a trip overseas," Dad had promised me at the start of the school year. When I heard that Dad was going to Israel, I asked him to keep his promise.

"But you haven't completed this school year yet."

"I know, but I don't think I'll have any problem making up for the missed days."

After a short discussion, Dad acquiesced. After he gave me the nod I was overwhelmed with joy. "I am going on a trip overseas! I am going to Israel!" I screamed, jumping around like a goat, and my delight filled the room to the brim. After calming down, I rushed to call Sue, my best friend.

"Sue, I'm going to Israel!"

"What … what do you mean you are going overseas, why?" she asked very excitedly.

I told her briefly. "And now I am getting ready for my trip to the promised land," I concluded happily. "Hey there, Sue, are you listening to me? Why don't you say something? Why are you being so quiet?"

"Okay, fine … have a good trip … goodbye!" she said and hung up.

What was going on? Why was she so angry? I remained silent all the way to Mamaroneck.

"Dan, why are you so quiet?" my father asked. "At home, you were dancing with joy and now you are dead silent. What happened? Do you want to tell me something?"

"I want to very much but …" I told Dad about Sue's strange reaction.

"Oh, now I understand," Dad said with amusement. "The lady disagrees. What do you want to do, give up?"

"Dad, I was thinking … can we take Sue with us?" I asked hesitatingly. "You know I have some money saved up and I'm ready to cover her expenses."

"I don't think you can afford that!" my father responded with laughter.

I was convinced that Dad would respond with a firm, clear "NO!", but instead, I was in for another surprise. "I am willing to take Sue with us, and to cover the costs," Dad said quietly. "But only with her parents' consent. If you can convince them to give their written consent, I would be happy to have her join us."

At first, Sue's parents refused to even listen to me, but after an entire week of begging and pleading, they agreed. A week later we were in a cab on our way to the airport. Soon the plane took off and we could see the Statue of Liberty receding further and further away from us until we could see it no longer.

My knowledge of the country we were headed to was limited to what I had seen on TV and read in newspapers. Only when we arrived in Israel would I realize how little I knew. By the end of this wonderful trip, I understood that Israel and its people were different from anything that I had ever imagined.

No, Israelis were not just a nation of soldiers. The cultivated lands showed that their knowledge of agriculture was excellent. The various industrial plants reflected a lively, prosperous, and modern country. The Holy Land did not seem to be the desert with caravans of camels all across it that I had expected to find.

Who are the Jewish people? Where did they find the courage to fight against so many enemies? What is the secret of their strength? I was sure many others had wondered the same things. These and other similar thoughts went through my mind as our airplane approached the Holy Land. I felt tired and dizzy. I gently placed my arm on Sue's shoulders and entered a world of dreams.

"Fasten your seat belts, please. We are about to land!" the pilot announced through the loudspeakers. The noise awoke me from my deep sleep. We landed safely, grabbed our bags, and made our way out of the airplane. On the tarmac, the sun's warm rays welcomed me. *A land blessed with sun,* I thought happily.

After a short security check, we left the airport and followed Dad's energetic pace. Then suddenly we heard a voice yelling at us in broken English. "Hey, sir! Need a taxi? I have an excellent service, something from the movies! I have air conditioning, 'tereo system with great American singers, Krank Sinatra, Julie Iglesias, Kirk Douglas, and many more. You are going to have a wonderful ride!"

We could hardly stop laughing at his supposed knowledge of American singers. But even if we had wanted to find another driver, we would have had a hard time getting away from this one. The driver was a huge man — about seven feet tall and perhaps 350 pounds. No other driver would dare to take us from this Big Bear.

Before Dad could say a word, Big Bear grabbed our two largest suitcases, raising them high. Soon we found ourselves hurrying up trying to follow the amicable driver who was galloping with our luggage towards his cab. People let the huge man — who growled at them, "Give way! Give way!" — by until we arrived at his taxicab parked at the entrance to the airport.

"Sir, listen to me, I want to help you … see? I think you need a good experience, ya? Ye should count on me, is going to make you great visit in Israel. You have a big head … with a lot of brains … I see you is smart. Ye come children too; ye gonna have a lot of fun."

After a brief moment, Dad gathered some courage and said, "My dear sir, we would be happy to travel with you, but I have a meeting at the hotel in Jerusalem in two hours and I need to prepare. Here is the address. Please go straight to this place."

"What you say, I do. Now we go to the hotel, but after … you go with me to Tiberias? You know *Tiberias*? Water … a lot of water in Tiberias. Or you want Jaffa? … Acre? Town is big … touristicus … with walls, big walls. You know the little Frenchman … the French king Goldman Bonaparte … he was strong … took over all of Europe. But not Acre … Acre was not good to him. Please we travel to see all of the cannons of the little man on the wall there."

However, Dad was already fast asleep in the cab's front seat and heard nothing of it.

Shortly afterward, we reached the hotel. Dad paid the fare, adding a tip for the timely service. When we reached the revolving door, our local art and history expert was still calling hoarsely, "Maybe you come with me like to see Caesarea, the town of Pharaohs' daughter … Pleopatra or Platforma?"

We didn't want to hear any more. To our great relief, the hotel door swiveled, and we rushed in. At last, we were protected from the wonderful offers of our history expert.

✡   ✡   ✡

After an expedient and welcoming check-in, we went to our rooms on the fifth floor, took a long shower, and … I fell sound asleep again.

Not long after I could hear Dad knocking on the door. "Dan," I heard Dad's voice, "I have that business meeting. I will be back in three hours. See you later."

A few minutes later, I didn't feel like sleeping anymore. I went through the door to the adjoining room and sat on the edge of Sue's bed. She looked like a sleeping princess. Her skin was as white as snow and her curly black hair made the contrast even sharper, adding beauty and charm.

We had first met at the school library, and since then, not a day had gone by without a phone conversation or a quick meeting. Sue was very charming. She knew how to listen, and, even if she didn't always agree with me, she expressed her objections quietly and gently. In Sue, I had found a true friend who could keep a secret and an intelligent friend who could give good advice. I was frequently amazed at her maturity. As far as I was concerned, Sue had opened up an unfamiliar and exciting world for me.

"Good morning, Sue," I whispered in her ear. "Good morning. It's time to consider our schedule again."

Sue opened her eyes, smiled, and said something in a somewhat sleepy voice.

"Sue, Dad went out to a meeting for a few hours, and I think this is our chance to go out and see the town without a police escort," I said half-jokingly.

"Great idea," said Sue. "But where are we going to go? We don't know this town."

"Let's go to the reception desk and ask. The hotel staff must know the town."

A good-looking receptionist welcomed us politely and answered all our questions about Jerusalem. Loaded with brochures, we sat in the lobby examining our options. What should we do? Where should we start our tour?

"Let's go to the Old City," Sue suggested. "I love old places."

So we caught a cab to the Old City. While riding I read one of the brochures:

The City of Jerusalem is Unique.

It is referred to by Israelis as "Jerusalem of Gold." Jerusalem has served as the capital of the Jewish nation for three thousand years, since King David, and all of its buildings are made of stone.

Today's homes are built the same. This building style adds beauty and charm to the city, which cannot be found anywhere else in the world. The well-known Temple was in Jerusalem. The Temple was destroyed twice and has never been rebuilt. Only a small part of the Western Wall is still there, reminding us of its past glory and opulence.

This city has known invaders and looters from all over the world: Assyrians, Babylonians, Persians, Greeks, Romans, Byzantines, Moslems, Turks, British, and many more. The conquerors of this city built memorials and buildings in memory of their triumph on the foundations of the Old City and the Temple. These memorials are still there.

The brochure filled my heart with a train of thoughts about the enchanting tour ahead of us and I felt very pleased that Sue had joined us. I knew we were about to have many marvelous experiences. I was still deeply absorbed in my thoughts as we reached the Old City.

Chapter 2

A Book or a Trap?

We got out of the cab and walked, hand in hand, along the long narrow alleys. Old stone houses surrounded by tall stone walls made it impossible for anybody to go through. We walked for a long time under the shadows of the tall walls. The sun could not penetrate into the long, narrow alleys. A mild wind spread a splendid scent. After a short while, we discovered the source of the scent: a stall at the entrance to a bakery.

We purchased some pita bread covered with a local herb-blend called *za'atar* and wondered about the slightly sour but also wonderfully gentle taste of the condiment. A few minutes later we continued through the narrow alleys, occasionally alarmed by calls of donkey riders whose warning to give way caused us to throw ourselves against the alley walls as they rushed past. Vehicles cannot pass through the narrow alleys, so all heavy loads must be carried by donkeys. We saw donkeys that could barely carry the loads on their backs, but their young riders would hit them with twigs, and the donkeys just jumped and kept walking with great effort.

"Sir … lady … please … this is a bargain!" A group of young peddlers seemed to appear out of nowhere and began following us. Within a few moments, they had us surrounded, telling us in broken

English about their excellent goods: soaps, shoelaces, razor blades, hairbrushes, and pictures of saints that could bring luck, wealth, happiness, and success — everything for little money, on a special sale. We continued through the alleys in this manner, surrounded by a chorus of youngsters shouting loudly, jumping around us, and presenting their goods.

At first, it was amusing to see how hard they tried to convince us that we had an unusual opportunity to buy exceptional goods at very low prices. However, after a while, the noisy group started to bother us. We pretended not to see them, but they would not leave us. We pretended to be deaf, but that didn't work either.

"There is nothing we can do," I told Sue. "We should walk faster and try to avoid them." So we started to walk fast, but the youngsters were just as fast as we were.

Eventually, we tried to lose them. We entered one of the stores as if looking to make a purchase and then we walked up and down the aisles, but our escorts did not give up.

We made one final attempt to elude the young boys hounding us by stopping at a small coffee shop just around the corner from the alley. We were already very tired, so we quickly sat down on two small stools. We drank our cold drinks, ate the honey-dipped cakes, and went back into the alley with our energy levels restored. After walking for a few minutes, we looked back and felt relieved. The young peddlers were no longer following us.

"Congratulations," said Sue, jumping around me like a chicken that has just laid her first egg.

But before she stopped jumping, another peddler suddenly appeared, following us like a shadow.

"Oh, to hell with him!" I exclaimed with disappointment, and we rushed ahead. But the peddler's voice could still be heard. "Holy water from the Jordan River. Holy water from the Jordan River ... sacred books, sacred books ..." We finally understood that we had no choice. We had to purchase something, or otherwise, we would never get rid of him. The moment we stood still, the peddler was already standing next to us with a mischievous smile on his face. He rapidly opened up a folding stall and took several volumes of the scriptures and a few bottles of water out of his bag for us to look at.

"Sir, everything is sacred!" he said with a serious expression. "Each of these items will bring you luck!"

Among his books, I saw a small book that looked quite worthless. *This is it!* I thought to myself. *I am going to buy this one book, and then I will get rid of this guy.*

I bought the book for two dollars without even examining it. As we walked away I said to Sue, "Throw it out into the first trash can you see. It can't be a holy book; it must be some silly rubbish."

We walked on for a while longer before deciding to head back to our hotel.

✡   ✡   ✡

When we got back to our rooms, I noticed that the book was still in her bag. "Sue, you forgot to throw the book away!" I laughed. "But you know what? Since you still have it, leave it so that I can see what we've bought."

After Sue retired to her room, I opened the book. To my surprise, I found that it was not a book. Instead, I saw a notebook or a diary written in handwriting that was totally unfamiliar to me. Strange drawings appeared on its last pages, something like a child's drawings. The pages at the end of the diary were empty.

"The young peddler sold us a used diary in a book cover!" I shouted angrily. "Mind, I can still use the empty ones for drawing." I pulled out my pocketknife and very carefully I tried to cut them out, but I couldn't do it. I tried again but the empty pages wouldn't tear off. Eventually, I checked the blade of my pocketknife. It was as sharp as a razor but against the booklet's pages, it didn't work. I pressed the knife against the pages, but it did not leave even the smallest mark on them.

"Hmm ... I have bought a magic notebook!" I muttered to myself. "If I can't cut the pages, then maybe I should just tear them off." I placed my foot over the diary and pulled the pages forcefully. Still, I could not tear them out.

I rushed into Sue's room to tell her about my sensational discovery.

"Dan, don't tell me ridiculous stories. I know you like teasing me, but please, I need to rest."

"But I am telling you the truth, in the name of all the white mice in the world."

"Oh, you really are funny," Sue mumbled sleepily.

"Usually I am funny, but this time I'm serious. Please come with me for just a moment!"

"Let's see what kind of a trick you have for me this time," Sue chuckled as she followed me through to my room.

There Sue took the diary and opened it. "It really looks like a diary to me. So what? You wanted to throw it out, so do it now. What's the problem?"

"Sue, it is impossible to cut this diary or tear it up."

"So what are you all excited about? It is probably just made of very strong stuff."

"What kind of stuff do you know that is similar to paper but cannot be cut?"

"I am not an expert in materials, but you can ask your father. He must know what it is. I have an idea — try burning this diary and then you'll see that it is nothing but paper."

"It's a great idea. Let's try to burn it in the shower."

"It is dangerous to burn it in the shower. It could start a fire."

"Don't worry. I will hold the showerhead ready."

I placed the notebook in the center of the bathtub and lit a match from the book of matches that I found next to the hotel stationary on the bedside table. For a moment it seemed that the match was about to start a flame, but it went out and the diary did not catch fire.

"These matches are not good enough to set the diary on fire," I said. "I will burn some of the hotel notepad sheets. That will get the fire going nicely."

"I think we should do it outside the hotel. I am afraid of fire."

"If you are afraid, and then why not go back to your room and I will do it by myself?" I said tersely. Sue said nothing.; she just stayed there next to me.

I lit the papers and placed the diary on them. I was convinced that this time the diary would burn. But it didn't. Instead, I saw an amazing sight; the diary glowed white-hot, yet it did not burn. We had seen nothing like this before. Sue, appearing shocked, said nothing for a while. Then she spoke up, "Dan, it really looks like somebody put us on. Maybe we should continue with this experiment outside the hotel."

"No, nothing will happen to us. Let's see how this diary ends up."

"I don't want to see. I am going to get some rest and I would appreciate it if you would stop this until your father returns." Sue departed, leaving me alone.

What should I do? I asked myself. I examined the diary further from all angles, but couldn't find anything special that could explain this mystery. All I knew was that I had to solve it! This time I gathered a lot more paper. I placed the diary on top and set the paper alight.

"I am sure that a larger fire will finish you off," I whispered to the flames that were rising upwards.

I looked at the diary and couldn't believe what I was seeing. It changed colors quickly, filling the bathroom with vibrant colors. Suddenly a thin, blue light beam came out of the diary and started to brighten the room. I stood there confused, feeling that something unusual was about to happen.

I have to put out the fire before there is any damage! I have to get a fire extinguisher! I quickly headed toward the door, and then — BOOM! A strong explosion made me fly toward the door, which was blown off its hinges, and we both sank onto the hallway floor. Circles of light and stars were moving in front of my eyes. I felt intense pain as if I had been hit by a baseball bat covered in nails.

The fifth floor was totally silent. Suddenly the doors of adjacent rooms opened and the faces of fearful people emerged.

"What happened? What is going on? What happened to the child? Call for help immediately!"

I could barely raise my head. My clothes were torn and covered in soot. My nose was bleeding. Black smoke was coming out of my room.

"Dan, what happened to you?" I heard Sue's anxious voice.

Before I could respond, two large men appeared. They put me on a stretcher and started running quickly to the elevator, Sue following close behind.

After a short ambulance ride, we reached the emergency room at a nearby hospital, where they put me on a bed. A few minutes later, a doctor appeared. After examining me thoroughly, he said: "You are a very lucky, young man. Other than mild wounds and some singed hair, there is nothing wrong with you. You just need some rest and we will take care of your wounds. Tomorrow morning you will be discharged."

About an hour later, Dad arrived at the hospital. "Dan, what happened to you? What caused the explosion?" he demanded nervously.

"I ... I don't know. The diary exploded."

"What do you mean, 'the diary exploded'? What diary exploded? Since when do diaries explode? Well ... look I understand you are still confused. We'll talk again tomorrow. In the meantime, you need to rest. I am glad you were not seriously hurt." Dad kissed me on the forehead, Sue gave me a shy hug, and then they both left the room.

The following day Dad arrived at the hospital early, accompanied by Sue, to take me back to the hotel. On our way back, he listened silently to my story about the explosion.

"Well," Dad said finally, "I really don't understand what happened to you, but please I am asking you to refrain from doing anything like this in future."

We went up to our hotel rooms. Amazingly my room appeared undamaged, the door had been remounted, the furniture must have been replaced, and there was no sign of any smoke damage from the explosion, even my personal effects appeared unharmed, Sue and I were confused. Dad went straight to his room to get ready to go out for his day of meetings. Almost immediately after Dad left the hotel, I heard three quick knocks on the door. "Come in," I replied, and opened the door. There stood a young man with short hair and a long mustache.

"Hello, young man," my visitor said. "I would like to talk to your father. There was no reply from his room. It is the request of the hotel manager."

"Sorry, my Dad went to work and won't be back until this evening."

"Well, then I am inviting you to meet with the hotel manager, who is extremely curious to hear what happened in your room last night. You will probably be able to explain the strange explosion, young man. Before you meet with the hotel manager, you'll also have to meet with the hotel's security officer."

"Aren't you also interested in what my friend Sue has to say?"

"No, there is no need for that. Hearing your side of the story will be sufficient."

I followed his footsteps down to the lobby and shortly afterward we arrived at a door with a sign that read 'Security' fixed on it. My companion knocked three times and waited. A loud voice replied, "Please come in." My companion pushed me forward lightly, saying sarcastically: "Don't just stand there like a beggar in the doorway. Here you are the guest of honor."

I stood in the doorway for a moment, and then, with some hesitation, I stepped right into the center of the room. A man of average height was standing in one corner, facing the wall. He turned around suddenly and looked at me, saying quickly, "Is that you, the nice kid who was playing with some sort of bomb? You blew up your room! Why? What was that supposed to be about? Do you think it's a kid game? Listen to me well, perhaps your father has a Ph.D., but you are probably crazy! Now, I want to know what happened. Tell me!"

I summarized my story very briefly. When I finished, he examined me for a long time and said, "It doesn't make any sense, but I will check it out. You can go now. Please go to the hotel manager; the young man outside will show you the way. I will tell him of your coming."

I found the hotel manager sitting behind a huge wooden desk in his office at the end of the hallway. I immediately noticed that this man was not your typical manager. His eyes were burning like a snake's and his teeth were screeching like the teeth of a starving tiger.

As soon as my companion closed the door and left, he jumped from his seat and stood in front of me, his teeth still screeching in anger. Then he screeched maliciously, "You little brat! What have you done to my hotel? Why are you experimenting with explosives in my hotel? Want to ruin me? You, you small damn varmint!"

His face became red as a tomato, his hands were trembling and his throat choked. "You are lucky … yes, you are lucky that I am a very nice and calm person," he continued. "I am a calm person," he repeated, his screeching voice rose up to unbearable decibels, his fists pounded on his desk. "What have you done to my hotel? Do you want to ruin my good reputation? Do you think I am going to believe the dumb stories that you told the security officer? Books exploding?" He continued to increase his loud and fiery shouts. "Take yourself and your father and get out of my hotel before I kill you with both my bare hands!"

As I saw him grabbing a large flower pot, I rushed toward the door. The moment I closed the door behind me, I heard a loud crash — the door nearly collapsed. A number of hotel employees were standing in the corridor near the door laughing quietly, but they quickly disappeared into other rooms as if the devil himself were chasing them.

My father returned late in the evening, and I immediately told him what had happened. He was angry about the hotel manager's stupid behavior and decided that we should move to another hotel. "I heard from my acquaintances at the conference about this Bernhard Boan, the craziest hotel manager in town. They were laughing at me when they heard about my choice to stay here."

A little while later Dad, Sue, and I walked out through the lobby and entered a cab that was waiting at the hotel entrance. I was very happy to leave the 'calm' hotel manager behind. I still don't know which was worse, the crazy hotel manager or the explosion.

✡   ✡   ✡

We arrived at a very fancy hotel in the western part of the city. After getting unpacked and resting for a while, Dad asked me, "Dan, can you tell me please, what exactly caused the explosion?"

I told him the entire story about our visit to the Old City, the purchase of the diary, the fire, and the explosion.

"I really don't understand this. How can a book or a diary explode? I am glad that nothing serious happened to you. From now on, don't buy anything that seems to be strange. Starting tomorrow I am going to be at the Weizmann Institute in Rehovot during working hours. I suggest that you take a tour of this beautiful country. I spoke to a travel agent and he made several suggestions for great tours. It is too bad that I won't be able to join you. There are some magnificent places and ancient archeological sites. Here is my phone number at the Institute. Take care of yourselves and we will meet when I get back in the evenings. Please make sure you don't do anything dumb. You are not a child anymore."

✡   ✡   ✡

When I saw Dad early the next day morning he said his goodbyes to me with a kiss and said, "Have a great time and stay out of trouble."

When Sue woke up, she informed me right then and there, "We should find a philologist."

"A philologist? Why?" I answered.

"I have a surprise for you. Open my handbag," she said mischievously.

I looked inside and saw the diary.

"This is impossible … how did you do it? It must have been burnt up in the explosion."

"When I heard the explosion, I rushed to your room and I saw you lying on the hallway floor. I could tell that perhaps you were slightly confused but otherwise, you seemed fine. The first thing I did was to remove the diary from the room and place it inside my handbag so there wouldn't be any evidence against you. Now it's time for us to find out the secret of this notebook. To do that, we need a philologist who will be able to decode it."

"Sue, I must say, you are fantastic. It is really about time that we find out more about this diary. I think we should go to the university and search for a philologist over there."

A few minutes later we caught a taxi. "To the City Center, please, and from there to the Hebrew University," I told the cab driver.

"Why the City Center?" asked Sue.

"I want to photocopy this strange diary and give a copy to the philologist. The original will remain with us."

Once we were in the cab, I took out the terrifying diary and examined it from all sides. The diary was intact. Not a single scratch nor a single singed page.

How is this possible? The diary exploded and burned, but still remains as it was before ... as if nothing happened to it! I flipped through the pages again and could not see anything that had changed. I searched my mind for all the events that I could remember, beginning with our encounter with the teenage peddler, who sold us the diary, to the huge explosion. But I could not recall anything that seemed significant.

✡   ✡   ✡

When we reached the Hebrew University, we asked one of the secretaries of the Hebrew Language Department where we could find a philologist. "And why do you need one?" she asked.

"I purchased a diary in the Old City written in a strange language, and we need a philologist to translate it for us."

"Children, I think you are searching in the wrong place. Our professors do not have the time to translate diaries. But you can try your luck with Professor Meir Alon." She lowered her voice. "He is here today, his office is in lecture hall no. 9 in this building. Please don't tell him I sent you."

A few minutes later, we knocked on the door of lecture hall no. 9, but there was no reply. "Maybe he is not in there," Sue whispered to me. "You never find them where they're supposed to be." She carefully opened the door and we peeped slyly inside. Shelves filled with books lined the large hall, but not a living soul was to be seen.

"There's no one here, let's go and come back later," Sue said.

Just as we were about to leave, we heard a cough. "There is somebody here. Look, there is another room," I said, pointing to a door slightly ajar at the far end of the hall.

Slowly we approached the half-opened door and saw the professor, sound asleep on his chair behind a large table loaded with books.

"Do not wake him up," Sue said. "He might be annoyed if we disrupt his siesta."

"I will not be annoyed," said the professor, opening two eyes full of laughter. "I simply let my eyes rest for a little while. My young friends, what has brought you here, to my room?"

I handed him over the diary pages and announced, "This photocopied diary intrigues me a lot and I'm looking for some answers about it."

The professor skimmed through the diary and asked, "What would you like to know? This is a simple diary, written in ancient Hebrew. This is probably the notebook of some student who is learning the language."

"Maybe, maybe not. This is not a regular diary," I said quietly. "I would like to tell you the story about how we came to acquire this diary. I must warn you that possibly my story will sound a bit strange, but this is the plain truth, and Sue here can confirm what I say."

"Excuse me, young friends, I haven't invited you to sit down yet, so please be my guests. Now listen to me, I have been through many unusual situations and heard many strange stories in my lifetime. Please try me — I'm eager to hear something fascinating and new. I'm all ears," he replied with a smile. Then he remained silent while I told my story. He kept his silence after I had concluded, and he looked like someone who was considering what to say next.

"My young man," the professor finally said, "I have to tell you that this story is as excellent as any science fiction book. But ... this kind of story exists only in fairy tales. I warmly recommend that you find out what caused the explosion in your hotel room. Perhaps there were some explosives inside the diary, and you were unaware of it when you purchased it. However, I like your story very much – it's really a nice one – and in order to satisfy my curiosity, I am willing to translate the diary for you. Please come back in three days."

I gave him the photocopied pages of the diary and we departed, to head back to our hotel.

"Maybe this diary is a trick device and was loaded with some explosive material between the pages," I told Sue as we sat in the back of the taxicab.

"No that's impossible," she pointed out. "The diary would have been blown to pieces."

"You're right, of course. What on earth happened?" I replied.

"We will know in three days," she said, "so don't jump to any conclusions."

"Three days is a long time. I don't really have the patience to wait three whole days."

"Let's tour the city and time will go by quicker," Sue suggested.

"I think I shouldn't have told the whole story to the professor. He is not going to take this matter seriously. He probably thinks we are just a pair of lunatics. He may just throw away the pages and tell us to forget about it, except that now he will have some new jokes about lunatics claiming that diaries somehow explode but stay intact."

We returned to our rooms feeling tense and preoccupied with our thoughts. *I hope the professor discovers something soon*, I said to myself.

The following morning we went for another walk around Jerusalem. We explored several of the enormous number of historical sites of the ancient capital of the Jewish people. When we returned to the hotel, we found a message waiting for us: "Please call Professor Alon urgently."

"I don't understand what could possibly be so urgent," Sue said.

"He probably found something interesting. The combination of ancient Hebrew and an exploding diary is not the most normal thing in the world after all," I answered with sheer enthusiasm.

Chapter 3

The Search for the Young Peddler

We grabbed a quick lunch, then called Professor Alon.

"Fantastic, I am glad to hear that you are on your way. Excellent! Please do not forget to bring the original diary with you. It is very important! Very important! See you soon! See you soon!" the professor said excitedly.

"Do you realize how excited the professor was? He's probably found something. I'm so happy," I said to Sue exuberantly.

✡   ✡   ✡

When our cab stopped in front of the university building, the professor was already there and hurried forward to open the cab door. "My esteemed friends, where is the diary, please?" he asked, out of breath. His excitement was contagious and I gave him the diary.

With his hand shaking and with a fixed look on his eyes he muttered, "Come to my room, please."

He walked toward his room briskly. We could hardly keep up with him. When we reached his room, the professor stopped immediately, gave us a brief sideways look, and then offered us some cold fruity drinks. "Sorry for my hurrying; I hope that something to drink will make for it". With an excited look on his face, he continued, "Dear friends, I would be happy to hear your entire story all over again. I did not listen too carefully last time, but now I will listen to each and every word. The mystery of this diary has captivated me. I'm all ears!"

I repeated the story about our visit to the Old City, the purchasing of the diary, and everything that had happened, leading up to the big explosion.

"This is a most amazing story, perhaps the strangest I have ever heard! There are many unusual things here that require a most thorough investigation," proclaimed Professor Alon. He picked up the diary and checked it very carefully "Incredible! There is no sign on this diary indicating that it had exploded or been thrown into a fire ... no sign whatsoever." The professor removed his glasses off, wiped the sweat off his brows, and with a magnifying glass he drew from his desk drawer examined the diary intently. "The material this diary is made of is unfamiliar to me. There are very strange designs drawn on it. Who wrote it? When? I would like you to do something very important — find that young peddler and ask him where exactly he got this diary. It is very important to know where he got it. And I, my young friends, will investigate the material of which this diary is made and the strange drawings on it. I should have some answers in one or two days.

"Before you leave," he continued, "I would like to tell you that we possibly have an internationally significant discovery on our hands. If it's true, you are going to be very famous, but in the meantime, we should keep it completely secret! No one should know about this diary. Not one word! Promise?"

"Promise!" Sue and I exclaimed together.

The next morning, when we left the hotel, we saw a cab waiting by the entrance with its cabby sleeping head forward on the steering wheel. Sue tapped gently on the window but he didn't move. I was more daring and knocked on the door, but we got no response from the fat-bellied driver. The driver didn't wake, only his big belly went up and down while the breaths that came from his gapped mouth sounded like a whale before diving to the ocean's depths.

"What's the problem?" a hotel guard asked us. "Oh, you want a cab? Don't worry, I am going to wake up the driver. I am going to fix this problem".

The guard opened the cab door and punched the cab driver with a decisive blow on his back. "I'm fixing the problem," he said with rolling laughter.

"Stop, what are you doing?!" Sue exclaimed crying sharply.

"I am fixing this problem. I fix this problem every single day," he concluded and started to bash the driver's head on the steering wheel.

I was standing dumbstruck. "Sir, Sir, you ... could kill him," I stuttered.

As the driver continued to sleep, the guard looked scornfully at me and said, "Now you are going to see my best and final trick, the kind of trick that would wake up even the dead!"

He pulled a black plastic bag out of his pocket and covered the driver's head with it.

"No!" Sue shouted, shaking like a leaf in the wind.

In a wink, the snoring stopped. The driver who looked like he is going to pass out suddenly jumped out of his seat and pulled the plastic bag off his head, muttering confusedly, "Oh, yes, yes ma'am, mister ... where to? Yes, children, nothing to worry about. Please enter, I am ready to move."

Only after we had recovered from our shock, did we get into the cab for our ride to the Old City.

"Sometimes I fall asleep and I don't wake up," the driver told us. "It makes me lose a lot of money. My luck is that the security guard is my good friend and you know what? He helps me a lot. Do you see the large ugly wound on my forehead? I got it as a gift last week. I was successfully awoken by someone hitting me with a big stick on my head. See, I had four irritated tourists that I took as passengers to the Judean desert, where I fell asleep. They could not wake me up in any other way after three hours and getting almost dehydrated from thirst. Do you understand what it means to be thirsty in the desert? My God, that was really some kind of waking up. A plastic bag is as gentle as a lamb comparing to all the other means. Angry passengers, you see?"

The driver repeated himself several times and finally cracked up laughing. His contiguous laugh made us laugh too, for the remainder of our journey into the Old City. After we alighted from the cab, we eventually stopped laughing and started to focus on the mission that was in front of us.

"How can we find the young peddler among so many people?" Sue asked.

"We are going to walk through the streets where we went during our first tour. You will check on the left side and I will check on the right. Let's go!"

A few minutes later we reached the place where we had initially seen the young peddler, but we saw nothing of him there. We continued walking through the narrow long alleys. Many peddlers were promoting their goods with loud voices, but we ignored them; advancing slowly as if the streets were empty.

After two hours of walking Sue, fatigued, declared: "Dan, I can't go on searching anymore."

"You are right, we'll continue tomorrow." I was happy to return to the hotel for a rest too. When we arrived, the receptionist gave me a note with the followings:

Hi Dan and Sue!

There's some urgent work that I need to complete at the Weizmann Institute. I apologize but I will be staying in Rehovot at a colleague's home for the next three days. Have a good time. In case you have any urgent problems, please call the number at the Institute and they will get ahold of me. See you soon.

Love, Dad

✡   ✡   ✡

The next morning, after rousing Sue from a deep sleep, I called Professor Alon and reported on our inability to locate the peddler.

The professor sighed in disappointment. "Too bad! You simply do not understand how unusual this diary is. I checked it for many hours and I have to tell you that you were right. I apologize for my skepticism toward you in our first meeting. I learned more about the diary, it is made of an unknown material. You told me that you set it on fire but it did not burn and even much more than that – it exploded. I've got to investigate this phenomenon.

"Listen, young man, what we have here is either an international sensation or a global deception. I am going to start experimentation with it, and if I am lucky, I will find an answer to this strange mystery. But until solving it, I urge you, go to the Old City and find the young peddler, please. He may have the link to solving this puzzle. Goodbye, and I hope to see you later with good news."

"An international sensation or a global deception!" I repeated the professor's words out loud. "Sue, let's get on with the detective work!"

"Dan, don't get too excited. What if we don't find him today too?"

Perhaps she is right, what then?

✡　✡　✡

The breeze that welcomed us as we reached the Old City was cool and soothing. The nice weather made me feel as if we were just strolling there rather than hounding after prey. I felt I was playing my cards right. A teenager on a donkey that passed next to us gave me an idea.

"Sue, maybe we too should ride a donkey so that we can keep going longer without getting tired."

She gave me a stern look and replied, "You know I cannot ride. I've never even sat on one before."

"Don't worry Sue. The owner of the donkey will walk alongside and hold it by its halter."

"OK, I'll give it a go," Sue responded immediately.

Shortly afterward we found ourselves two donkeys for hire. At first, Sue looked very stressed but several minutes later she began riding the donkey as if she had been born on one, and even joked about her prior fears. After a long ride, we reached a large square, crowded with people. Looking around, I noticed a familiar figure at the far end of the square. The young peddler!

"Sue, there he is!" I called out with glee. Immediately we jumped off the donkeys and ran toward him.

The young peddler was busy selling a variety of his merchandise and did not see us approaching him.

"Hi," I said calmly, placing an arm on his shoulder.

The peddler turned around, recognized me, and started a fearful cry, "It wasn't me! I didn't do it! Please, leave me alone!" His frightened calls attracted many people who watched the scene with curiosity.

"What is he afraid of?" Sue asked.

An old man came out of the crowd. He approached the teenager and spoke to him in an unknown language. He then turned to us and said, "Tell me, please, what do you want from the boy? Let's go somewhere away from all these people."

We followed the old man and the boy down to a street corner. When we could no longer see the crowd, the old man lowered his voice and asked, "What do you want?"

I told him quickly about the strange diary and the professor's request without mentioning the explosion.

"Please dear visitors, my home is over there, in the Wadi[1] going down between those two hills. Please come and be my guests. We will talk quietly and respectfully, and you will hear the story about the diary."

The old man went down the Wadi in the direction of his house as quickly as a young boy; we could barely keep up with him.

"Wow," I said to Sue, breathless. "This old man is really fit. Look how fast he runs. Unbelievable!"

The old man had a two-story house surrounded by piles of junk. He knocked on the door three times, yelling to his wife. A moment later the door opened. An old woman stood at the entrance, welcoming us with a broad smile. We followed the old man up to the second floor of the house. Though it didn't have much furniture, the house was

---

[1] Wadi is an ephemeral stream

clean and spacious with many old rugs that were covered by timeworn and colorful sitting bolsters.

"Please sit down," the old man said. "My wife will soon serve you with refreshments and hot coffee."

The young peddler left the room and returned with a water pipe, called a Nargila. The teenager lit the coals, and the old man started inhaling from the long pipe, blowing smoke.

"Now we can talk. First, tell me who you are," the old man inquired.

"My name is Dan, and this is my friend Sue. We are tourists from the United States. We are visiting with my father who was invited as a scientist to attend a conference at the Weizmann Institute," I said briefly.

"Good," said the old man. "Now, I am going to tell you a little about myself. I am a descendant of the Jacobian family that has lived in this city for many generations. A few years ago, my brother and his wife were killed in a car accident and since then I have adopted their boy as my son. I can see that you want to know how the boy got the diary that you bought. Can you tell me why you are so interested to learn about the origin of the diary?" The old man inhaled again intensely from the Nargila pipe.

I repeated the entire story about the diary that I couldn't set on fire but this time I added the story of the explosion. At first, the old man seemed really surprised, but I sensed that he did not believe a word that I said.

"Young sir, I can't figure it out – it is impossible that the diary was set in a fire, sorry exploded … but stayed intact. Perhaps you had taken something before? Your story sounds a little strange, a fairy tale from the land of fairy tales," he said with a smile and scratched his scalp.

A good-looking girl dressed in a flowered robe entered the room and, without saying a word, laid a tray on the floor with three small cups of black coffee and honey-soaked cookies

"Please help yourself and taste the excellent coffee my daughter made," the old man said. He lifted the tiny cup of coffee and started sipping it loudly. "Aha! This is excellent! This is excellent!" he repeated loudly.

When I witnessed the joy with which he sipped his cup of coffee, I took a long sip too. Many years have passed since that day and the taste of that coffee is still with me. It was the most bitter coffee I have ever drunk. It was terrible! The coffee tasted so bitter that I thought poison would probably taste better. I could hardly stop myself from jittering in place and I reached out to grab some of the sweet cookies on the tray, pushing them hurriedly into my mouth.

"I see that you don't really like my coffee," the old man said, smiling.

"It's excellent," I exclaimed, "but few cubes of sugar wouldn't hurt."

"My friend Dan," the old man said, "I am going to ask the boy if he is willing to tell you how he got the diary."

The old man turned to the boy and they talked for a few minutes, again in that unfamiliar language. He then turned to me and said, "The boy is willing to tell you the story, but on condition that you keep everything he tells you a secret."

We nodded in agreement. The boy had left the room, only to return with a jug of cold water. "Please have a drink," the old man said. "You must be very thirsty."

He continued, "I just asked the Armenian-speaking boy what and how he found the diary. Well, I'm going to translate every word of his story. Probably you are unfamiliar with the boy's story, but I can tell you that he is very concerned about the thieves chasing him."

"What do you mean?" I asked with obvious surprise.

"My esteemed friend, when you hear the story, you will understand why he is so apprehensive. But remember, this story is the boy's secret and we shouldn't talk about it to anyone else."

The boy started telling his story in Armenian, and the old man translated his words into English.

Chapter 4

The Young Peddler's Story

A few days ago a dignified-looking man appeared in the Old City. The man marched through the alleys, walked down the wadis, climbed the surrounding hills, checking into every corner, as if he was searching for something. The man didn't even look at the peddlers, who tried on him their well-known tricks to no avail. He didn't buy anything. When they asked him if he wanted anything, he wouldn't respond.

At dusk when darkness came, he disappeared; no one was able to tell where to. The following day, at sunrise, the stranger reappeared and continued his search. Three days later, all the peddlers knew about the stranger.

Rumor had it that the man was insane, a lunatic, or maybe even the devil. Why is he here? Why is his black briefcase handcuffed to his wrist? What is it in the briefcase? Perhaps he is a spy or an archeologist? Who is he and what is he looking for?

Five days later in the evening, I went out to buy sugar in a nearby store. I suddenly saw the stranger walking a few steps ahead of me with a group of young boys strung out behind him. I was able to recognize the bunch of 'respectful guys' among them and immediately sensed that they were not following him without good reason. So, I followed at a safe distance behind them.

The stranger did not seem to be interested in the group following him. Anyway, he continued to walk down the long alley and he would occasionally stop to check the curbstones on the sidewalks. Everybody just knew the 'respectful thieves' of the Old City, but daren't say anything against those 'kings of the town'. My heart pounded while I followed. I could easily hear them talking from where I was. One said, 'There must be some good money in that black briefcase.'

At the head of the procession marched the 'Chief of Thieves', who is a well-known figure throughout the city, a huge burly man who wore an incredible mustache. I paused because I could tell that that something was about to happen, and I wasn't wrong.

When the stranger reached the corner of the alley, all four 'respectful guys' jumped at him, grabbed his arms and legs, and quickly cut the chains of the handcuff with a large pair of bolt cutters – then they fled with the snatched briefcase in their hands. Everything happened so quickly that I froze bewildered for a moment, but then I gathered my wits and galloped after them.

After a few minutes, the thieves stopped their flight near a narrow pathway going down to the wadi. I stopped too, then followed them as they carefully descended. Tall, wild shrubs grew from both sides of the path. The thieves walked a few steps and then bent down to see whether anybody was following them.

Luckily, I bent down a moment earlier and they did not notice me. I realized the tense silence in the area. Only the sound of crickets, that began chirping again, passed through the air. But they quit again a few minutes later when the troop of thieves stood up and continued moving. I was stressed to the limit but stepped carefully in their wake, with my knees trembling, my back bent. After a short walk along the path, they reached a half-ruined antiquated house and disappeared inside it.

For a few long moments, I sat there motionless. Then I got down on my hands and knees and progressed forward carefully. I held my breath occasionally and timidly pricked up my ears. In the dark, the demolished house looked like an ancient monster. The sound of the crickets intensified my stress and I approached it hesitantly with great fear. I was tempted to run away, but I thought to myself, *No, I shouldn't run away. Only cowards run away and I am not a coward!*

The sky darkened further as the sky was covered by clouds; the dim starlight disappeared. The noise of the crickets became sharper as if warning me of impending danger. And then I was at the entrance to the building. Slowly and trembling I went through the doorway and walked down the staircase, step by step until I saw only a short distance from me a ray of light penetrating from a keyhole.

My sense of fear vanished quickly and was replaced by great curiosity. *What are they doing in there?* I stood there tense for a long time.

Looking through the keyhole, I was able to see the 'respectful thieves'. They were sitting in the center of a large room, lit by the bright white light of a kerosene lamp. The room was filled with stolen goods: gilded chandeliers that hung from the ceiling, beautiful drawings, gilded statues, chinaware, and many more beautiful objects.

The four 'respectful' ones were sitting on large pillows on top of an amazingly magnificent Persian carpet and in its center, I could see the black briefcase.

"Who can guess what's in the black briefcase? Make a bet. Winner takes all! Cowards, place your bets," the chief shouted loudly, his mustache was shaking with excitement.

"Let's do it! We are going to make a bet!" two of the thieves yelled. They drew a large number of precious stones and stunning jewelry from their pockets. "The great betting is about to begin," they claimed with elation.

"The third 'respectful thief', a short guy with a thin imperial mustache, stood up and said, "I am not going to bet. I once saw a movie about a black briefcase of a spy. When the briefcase was opened, it exploded. Boom!" It seems that his tale put a dampener on their reveling joy and excitement. The two thieves suddenly were quiet.

"What's the matter with you? This little nut is blowing your mind with stories about movies and you, like two nerds, believe him? He probably wants the briefcase for himself. I once saw a movie about a burglar who gave a lot of money to his wife in the morning. In the evening nothing was left … the lady had spent it all. He worked so hard all day long or a whole week, and she spent it all in one go. These days, it doesn't pay to be a burglar." The chief cracked up laughing. "Today, it doesn't pay to rob a bank. Today, it is better to own a bank.

"Come on, don't be mice," he went on. "Place your bets. Who can guess what's in the briefcase? Get on with it! Place your bets!" Finally, as no one responded to him, he announced scornfully, "I am opening the briefcase! Anybody scared can go and hide in the other room." He pulled a big screwdriver out of his pocket and pushed it through the briefcase's lock until it popped open.

The chief put his hand into the briefcase probing inside it slowly. He pulled his hand out of the briefcase, holding a gilded box decorated with beautiful pictures between his fingers. "I want some money, I want a treasure!" he sang loudly.

Holding the box with his left hand, he very slowly lifted the lid and carefully put his hand inside it. A terrible "Ahaaaaaaaa!" was dreadfully emitted from his mouth.

The other three thieves froze like stuffed animals in a museum. By the time they regained their senses, their chief was lying on the floor, contracting with convulsions, foam spewing out his mouth. Then he suddenly stretched out; then moved no more.

The horrifying scene shocked the gang and as one man they started to lament. "Dead! He is dead! There are devils and evil spirits in the box!" Their screams frightened me so severely that my knees started to shake.

Suddenly one of the thieves raced toward the door yelling, "There are devils in this room. I am not staying here even one more minute." I barely had time to move before the door opened. "Ahaaaaa!" This time the scream was coming out of my mouth as I saw the thief immediately in front of me.

My terrified scream made the other two gang members jump and with a fearful cry, they raced to the door. When they saw an image as I stood in the dark by the door, they screamed even louder and rushed past me, up the stairs and a moment later they disappeared from my sight.

I have no idea how long I stood there paralyzed with fear before I collected myself and entered the room.

From a distance of four steps, I saw the chief lying on his back. His wide-open eyes staring at the ceiling.

I looked for the box. I was very curious to find out what it was in the box that killed the Chief of Thieves. I searched all the corners of the room but couldn't find it. Where had it gone?

I asked the dead Chief of Thieves with a laugh, "Maybe you could tell me where the box is?"

Before completing my answer, I suddenly saw his hand move. I immediately stood up terrified, but then I saw the devil — a small snake of yellowish-brown color that slithered from under the dead man's hand. I lifted a large flower pot and crushed the snake's head with one blow.

Now I was no longer fearful. *The box must be under the dead man's body*, I thought. I could hardly move the huge corpse. But indeed I found the box underneath it. Then very carefully I opened it. I looked inside … and saw the diary. I threw it on the floor and started to laugh loudly.

Unbelievable! A shabby booklet in such an elegant case … locked up in a briefcase and handcuffed to the stranger's wrist? Wait a minute, I pondered. No one would have kept a worthless booklet in such a beautiful box. Perhaps this diary is a special priceless one. Perhaps it's a diary of a spy? If this is so, who can tell me what is its value? I must run from this place – the 'respectful thieves' might recover and return to their den.

I lifted the diary from the floor and ran home quickly. I was exhausted when I arrived, took a long gulp of water, and after I calmed down I turned to my uncle and asked for his advice. I told him the entire story and handed him the diary.

My uncle peered at me lengthily and said, "My dear boy, you acted as if you were a crazy person! I'm afraid to even imagine what might have happened to you if the thieves had not panicked?" He turned the pages of the booklet and continued, "This type of script reminds me of ancient Hebrew letters. We shouldn't sell it during the coming month because the gang of thieves might return to their den, find the empty case, and start to search for you because they might have recognized your face. Now, dear son, my command is that for three days you are to stay at home. In the case that they do not come to look for you, it might signal that they did not see your face and then you'll be free to go about your work in the town."

My uncle kept me in the house for three days, one night I was awakened by the thuds of a spade. I jumped from my bed and from the window I could see my uncle burying the diary in the garden. I could not sleep that night. The scenes were racing in my head again and again. The opening of the black briefcase … the fumbling hand of the chief… pulling the gilded box inside it out, and then the opening of the box … the terrible yell, the dying chief and a dancing serpent under his palm.

"My uncle is wrong," I kept saying to myself. "This is not a simple diary; this is a diary of a spy."

In the morning, when my uncle went to work, I took the diary out of its place and decided to find a buyer for it. *I will probably find someone who will know how to appreciate its unique value*, I thought to myself.

At first, I tried my luck with the many tourists, but unfortunately, no one bothered to even take a look at it. Two days went by and no one was interested. I then decided to sell it at any price so that I will not have to see it anymore. You bought it for a few dollars.

The boy's story ended.

"Please Sir, with your permission," I said to the old man. "We request that the boy join us tomorrow when we visit the professor's office."

"I will let him go with you," said the old man, "on condition that you keep your promise and have him return home safely."

I shook the old man's and the boy's hands and we returned to the hotel.

✡   ✡   ✡

At sunrise, I woke up excited and tense, thinking of what was about to happen. I called Professor Alon to tell him about our meeting with the boy.

"It sounds very interesting," said the professor. "The story is getting complicated. Now we have to find the stranger, the owner of the diary. Perhaps he could tell us the meaning of the strange designs inside."

"Professor, we'll be with you in exactly two hours with the boy in tow. You'll be able to ask him what more he knows then."

"Yes, certainly. I am waiting for you."

"Professor, what about the diary? What have you discovered?"

"Yes, I am preparing a translation into English. This is a fascinating story about a creature arriving from a far-away planet, billions of years ago, and, as far as I understand, the creature is still here today."

"You're joking? Billions of years ago and you're telling me that this person is still alive?"

"I don't have a clear answer to that question yet. I am only getting started. We obviously need to conduct some more research before we know the actual answer. As I told you before, my young friend, there are two possibilities: either this diary is an international discovery or a global deception."

"Professor Alon, do you really believe that a creature from another planet can live for so long, stay here on Earth and that nobody knows about it?"

"My esteemed friend, we still live in a very primitive world. Three hundred years from now, today's best scientists will be considered as primitive people that had borne some ridiculous ideas. Everything is going to change entirely. Our acclaimed professors of medicine will not be accepted to work at a slaughterhouse. The knowledge we currently have will become totally obsolete and of little scientific value. And now, go and get the boy. We must have his help in finding the stranger."

Sue and I took a cab to the Old City and then walked to the young peddler's home. We could see him from far off, sitting at the entrance, waiting for us. He ran quickly up the wadi to welcome us and gestured for us to follow him. "Come," he said in broken English. "Please come."

We went down the wadi following the boy, but this time he didn't go in the direction of his home. "Where are we going now?" Sue asked me. We found ourselves about fifty meters from the boy's home, in front of a big house surrounded by a stone wall with a large green gate at the entrance. The boy knocked six times and waited. A tiny window opened on the second floor. A veiled woman peeked out for a moment and immediately shut the window. Then the green iron gate opened, and we saw a tall, thin man dressed in a silk robe and wearing strange slippers.

The man glanced at me, shook my hand, and said in good English, "Welcome. My name is Katolipus son of Eucalyptus, a descendant of a famous dynasty. My family has been living here for hundreds of years."

"I don't see why we have to listen to all the dynasty nonsense of this elegant peacock," Sue whispered in my ear.

"I don't either. Perhaps something meaningful is going to happen, so let's be patient. The boy seems to know why we are here and he knows what interests us."

The man led us to the balcony and invited us to sit on large bolsters that were placed on the floor adjacent to its concrete parapet. A tall concrete wall surrounded the house. We saw an immense collection of junk in the backyard — piles on piles that consisted of: rusty iron beds, empty bottles in different sizes, eroded wooden poles, empty tins, and more.

"Sir has a large yard," I said politely.

My host responded with a heavy sigh. "This is a very small yard. My family has been living here from before the times of the Ottoman — the Turks — who came here about four hundred and sixty years ago.

"The same day the Ottomans came here they stole from us of a lot of lands as they did from our Jewish neighbors. And so the good years gave way to bad times, when robbers from the desert invaded, again and again, and looted our lands, grabbed by force our children and the yields of our vineyards. Then built their homes on our stolen lands. I am very happy that the Jewish people returned to their land from the Diaspora and fought against the terrible, murderous invasions of the brigands from the desert with great bravery and eventually rebuilt their country."

Mr. Katolipus paused and took a gulp of water. He then embarked on a long, boring speech about his grandfather, father, brothers, cousins, and the entire long dynasty of his family. He didn't show any sign that his story would ever come to an end.

Sue whispered again to my ear. "Why must we stay listening to this chatterbox."

"I know. We need to take the boy to the professor and that he's waiting for us, but I don't have the slightest idea why we were brought here. Let's give this a few more minutes to play out."

Finally, our host stopped his long speech. "You probably realize that I have only begun to cover the story of my wonderful ancestry. However, I understand that you are in a rush. I would be happy to continue my fascinating story anytime after the meeting. I was very happy to talk to you."

"Meeting? What meeting?" I asked surprised.

"I did not bring you here for nothing. I have a surprise for you."

"Surprise? What kind of surprise?"

"Finally, something interesting is going to happen here," Sue whispered.

"You will soon meet the mystery man — the stranger."

"What? The stranger?" I exclaimed with excitement. "How could that be?"

"Why are you surprised? The entire Old City has already heard of the strange person called 'The Stranger'. You probably can understand how this man was seen as a remarkably unusual presence in our area."

Mr. Katolipus, the son of Eucalyptus, stopped lecturing as he saw his wife entering the balcony with a tray full of goodies. It seemed as if he was suddenly forgetful of both his lineage and good manners. He placed both hands in the middle of the tray and filled his big mouth with the cakes and biscuits, saying, "Don't be shy, use your hands and eat … eat, it's good."

Sue and I looked fascinated at our host, who kept swallowing food like a pelican. But then three loud knocks on the iron gate made our host stand up and look towards the entrance gate. He immediately called the boy and whispered something in his ear.

"Wow," Sue said. "Now we will finally be able to know who the mysterious stranger is."

I agreed with her and reflected on how wonderful this surprise would be for Professor Alon if we could bring the stranger along with us too. The boy's uncle, Mr. Jacobian, came up the stairs. Following him was a man of very impressive, exciting appearance and I became thrilled when I saw him.

"Please let me introduce you to Mr. Arthur D'Acosta," he said. Introductions completed, our host rushed to the kitchen and returned with a fresh tray of goodies. I looked at the stranger's face, wondering whether I would now hear the secret of the diary.

Arthur D'Acosta was a young man of about twenty-five, six feet tall, his black hair neatly combed back. His face was calm as that of a prince. He wore a small adhesive bandage on his forehead, most probably the result of meeting the town's 'respectful' thieves in the fight over his briefcase. His right forearm was encased in a big white bandage. But his injuries did not detract from his noble looks.

Mr. Katolipus rushed to his room and immediately returned with a new, very elegant, silk robe.

"What's the matter with this peacock?" Sue whispered in my ear. "Why is he dressed up like that?"

"He is probably getting ready for a new show," I winked to Sue.

Mr. Katolipus raised the loaded tray and asked his guests to taste his wife's delicacies. This time he didn't stuff himself as before. As his guests filled their mouths, Mr. Katolipus resumed his boring account of the genealogy of his family and how its ancestry goes back to an earlier period than the Ottomans.

Sue did not miss the opportunity; she leaned her head on my shoulder and started to nap. Since I had heard this show earlier, I leaned back to the wall behind me, closed my eyes. Before dropping off, I could see the peddler boy trying hard not to fall asleep. His eyelids were fluttering until he finally gave in.

I have no idea how long it was before the boy's voice woke me up again. He touched my shoulder, saying "Mr. Dan!" I opened my eyes and saw that the boy was busily trying to wake his uncle up too.

I was pleased to see that Mr. Katolipus was no longer on the balcony. I immediately seized the opportunity to talk to the mysterious stranger, Mr. Arthur D'Acosta.

But before I could open my mouth, the stranger spoke to me. "Young man, tell me please if you have my diary."

I told him briefly what had happened to the diary from the day I purchased it until that moment. The stranger then stood up and said, "I will be happy to meet with you and the professor at my hotel tomorrow morning at nine o'clock. Please bring the diary with you." He wrote down the name of the hotel, shook Mr. Katolipus's hand, who had just rejoined us, and left. We took the opportunity to say goodbye to our hosts and returned to our hotel.

✡   ✡   ✡

When we entered the room, I rushed to the phone and called Professor Alon to tell him about the surprising meeting with the stranger.

"What?" the professor exclaimed in a loud voice. "The stranger is a member of the D'Acosta family? Do you know who this family is? This is a very well-known family of Marranos from Spain."

"And what are Marranos?" I asked with curiosity.

"This is a very long story. I will try to tell it briefly. About five hundred years ago, the Jews of Spain were expelled by the king and the queen of Spain. Jews wishing to remain in Spain had to convert to Christianity. Many families did not want to leave the country where they had been living for hundreds of years. So these families had to convert. Many Marrano families[2] continued to follow their Jewish religion in hiding. It was kept a secret. Anybody caught following the Jewish religion secretly was tortured by the church emissaries. Many times, the victims were burned to death in town squares."

"I still don't understand the connection between the diary and Arthur D'Acosta's heritage," I said to the professor, but I didn't receive an answer.

"Young man, tomorrow at exactly 8:40 we will meet at the entrance of your hotel and we will then go to Arthur D'Acosta's hotel."

The following day I woke up from my deep sleep thinking about the upcoming meeting with the mysterious man, Arthur D'Acosta. I struggled with so many questions – *why was the diary guarded using a snake and what was he searching for in the Old City?* These burning questions made me all the more so stressed on the one hand and curious on the other hand, and you can probably imagine yourself how it felt. At exactly 8:40 a.m. the professor arrived at the hotel parking area where Sue and I entered his dilapidated old car that chugged like a tractor and left a trail of black smog behind it.

"Good morning, esteemed friends! I'm very excited about our meeting. Please put your safety belts on – we are taking off! We must not be late!" Then he pressed the gas pedal to the floor. The professor drove frantically. "We shouldn't be late," he mumbled.

The city sights seemed to be passing so quickly viewed from the window of our fidgeting and smoking car as we climbed uphill. I prayed to God that this crazy trip would end before the old car fell apart.

---

[2] Marrano means pig. It was the poignant epithet given to Jews who were made to hide their religion by the Inquisition in Spain.

We arrived at D'Acosta's hotel five minutes before nine. Sue got out of the car swaying as if she'd just emptied a full mug of draft beer and sat herself down in the hotel lobby to recover.

"I hope that Mr. D'Acosta is punctual," the professor said, taking the diary out of his jute bag. "Look at the strange drawings here. I think this is a map of a very ancient city. It shows paths and strange designs of a very large building. It is possible that our friend D'Acosta was looking for something on this map and perhaps he will be willing to tell us what he's looking for. But it is also possible that he is merely an archeologist or an antique robber. I am refraining from revealing my findings to other researchers since this could be either an international discovery or a global deception. I have to be careful ..."

"Professor, what's written in the diary?" Sue interjected.

"Yes, this strange diary. This is the diary of a very special person telling an unusual story. I don't know whether his story is true or if it is just an inflated account of the truth onto which have been grafted some unusual ingredients to spice it up.

"The diary tells about a creature arriving from the faraway planets called the Seventh World. According to a Jewish belief, our cosmos is divided into Seven Worlds with Seven Skies, and the story of the diary is very similar to the tenets of the Jewish religion.

"I have to tell you that, from the moment you gave me the diary, I have hardly slept. I'm overwhelmed by so many questions. Who wrote this diary? Who is D'Acosta and what is he looking for in the Old City? From what material is the diary made of? Many questions remain unanswered. Without getting a few answers from the stranger my research might stay incomplete."

At that moment, Mr. D'Acosta arrived, he advanced straight to our table and introduced himself to the professor. He then turned to us and said, "I would appreciate it if you let me know what you would like to be given as a reward for returning my diary?"

The professor said, "Mr. D'Acosta, we don't want a reward for returning your diary; we want only a few answers for some questions about this amazing diary."

The professor told the foreigner everything he knew about the diary and asked a few of the battery of questions he had in hand.

Mr. D'Acosta picked up the diary and turned its pages briefly. "I am very pleased to see my stolen diary returned to me, and obviously I'm very grateful for everything you've done for me. I hope I will be able to reward you one day for all your incredible efforts. Unfortunately, I have to leave now. There is a very important task I must complete it, and then I will be very happy to meet again and tell you my story. I beg you again to excuse me." Having concluded he stood up and turned to leave the hotel.

"Mr. D'Acosta, please excuse me but I must get a few answers about your extraordinary diary in order to continue my research on it. You owe me a few answers at least."

"Professor Alon, unfortunately, I can't give you any more information until my mission has been completed, then I will. And again thank you so much for returning my stolen diary. Goodbye, and I hope to see you again!"

Mr. D'Acosta's sudden departure left us confused. It was an unexpected ending to such an anticipated meeting. I can hardly describe the look of shock on Professor Alon's face after D'Acosta's hasty exit. He sat motionless like a Buddha for several minutes.

"What are we going to do now?" I asked the professor, but he didn't respond. He just sat there upright, his eyes opened wide, his mouth gaped. After he recovered he mumbled, "I am very tired. Let's go home!"

This time the professor drove very slowly. There was a deafening silence in the car. No one uttered a word.

When we arrived at the hotel, the professor stopped his car and said, "Tomorrow at 5:00 a.m. we are going to surprise Mr. D'Acosta at his hotel. I think he owes us a few answers and I have no intention of giving up so easily."

The professor started his car again and disappeared followed by a trail of black exhaust fumes.

✡   ✡   ✡

As we took the elevator I asked Sue, "Do you think Mr. D'Acosta is going to reveal his secret to us?"

"I don't think so. The professor is wrong. Mr. D'Acosta is a very imposing man and he is not going to give in."

"I agree with you. Mr. D'Acosta can reveal his secret any time if he wants, and I believe that his position should be respected."

We decided to spend the rest of the day exploring the area around the hotel, enjoying the plentiful sunshine, and perusing the local shops and eateries. Of course, the diary was always on our minds, dominating our discussions. We had so many questions for Mr. D'Acosta and the professor both.

✡　✡　✡

Exactly at 5:00 in the morning, the professor arrived at our hotel. We sat in the back, clinging fast to our seats. The professor looked awful and after saying our good morning we sat quietly with our mouths shut. When we arrived at Mr. D'Acosta's hotel, the car stopped with a squealing from its brakes, and the professor got out entirely agitated, and then he announced, "I am going to catch the evader!" He hastily entered the reception hall; Sue and I followed him.

"Sir, good morning," the professor addressed a sleepy receptionist near his desk. "Could you please let Mr. D'Acosta that his friends are waiting for him in the lobby?"

The sleepy receptionist checked the guest list and called D'Acosta's room. The phone rang for a long time but nobody picked it up.

"I am sorry, there is no answer," said the receptionist.

"What do you mean there is no answer? What is Mr. D'Acosta's room number?" the professor asked.

"Room number forty-three, fourth floor," the sleepy receptionist replied.

The professor sprang forth and raced up the stairs to the fourth floor. "Room forty-three, fourth floor... room forty-three, fourth floor," he chanted while storming up the stairs.

We were still on our way there when we could hear the professor's strong knocks on the door of room forty-three. Due to the noise, people were peeking into the corridor from some of the nearby rooms,

47

but the professor continued to knock on the door loudly. It took him a few minutes to give up and run back downstairs to the reception desk. We followed him.

"Sir, could you please open the door of my friend, Mr. D'Acosta? I am very concerned that something might have happened to him."

The receptionist apologized and then called the hotel manager. After a short conversation, he said, "Sir, come with me, please. I will open the door for you."

When we arrived at the door of room forty-three, the receptionist knocked on the door several times, put his ear close to the door in an attempt to hear if there was anyone in the room, and eventually used the key.

The professor pushed through even before the door was fully opened and charged into the room. "The slippery eel has escaped!" the professor exclaimed angrily. "He did not even sleep here last night, the bastard. His bed is made! Why should I continue to waste my time on such a slippery individual? I announce here and now that my investigation of the diary is hereby finished. Sorry, the case is closed. Unless you bring me new evidence, I wash my hands of it."

✡   ✡   ✡

When we arrived back at our hotel again, the professor took a large envelope out of his bag and handed it to us, saying, "This is the translation of the diary. I am telling you goodbye now. If you ever visit the Holy Land again, remember to visit me. So long."

At the entrance to the hotel, I smiled and asked Sue, "What do you think about the angry professor?"

"I think he was overly-aggressive. He lost his patience too quickly. The bright side of this is that we have the translation of the diary. Perhaps it will help us learn something about our unsolved mystery."

Chapter 5

The Diary

"Sue, let's read the translation together. Who knows, perhaps together we can find some answers." Sue sat at the table in my room and started to read the first page out loud. Soon we sank entirely into another world.

Preface to the Translated Diary

By Professor Meir Alon, Hebrew University, Jerusalem – May 10, 1968

This is an accurate translation of a diary that I received from Dan and Sue, two American tourists. I did not add or revise anything in it. The diary was written by a member of the ten lost tribes of Israel during the period shortly after they were exiled from their homeland, about two thousand and seven hundred years ago. In his diary, the author tells about a mysterious being that appeared in a huge cavern that he and the ten lost tribes shared, which he dubbed The Hovering Being. This being told the author that it came from a planet that is immensely distanced from Planet Earth. Is the author's story a beautiful legend or a true story? I do not know for sure. Right now, all I have is this accurate translation of the diary without any revisions or added interpretation of my own. It is presented to you here below:

The Diary of Zvi Ben Yosef

I, Zvi Ben Yosef, the scribe and member of the family of the ten deported tribes of Israel, swear by God and by my ancestors' honor that everything written in this book is the absolute truth and not just legends. I have received each and every word which is written in this book from the Hovering Being which appeared in the cavern, and I have kept my writing faithful to my source.

I have now completed the writing of the three books. The Hovering Being declared that those books cannot be destroyed either by fire, water, or force. No one will ever be able to destroy them! I am going to hide these three books in the Great Cave so that my secret will not be revealed to my brothers, members of the ten tribes. I am aware that my brothers, members of the ten tribes, might harm me and my family if they were to find these books, and therefore I will hide them in some secluded places. I am positively sure that, one day the three books will be found by mankind… and then the world will change to a great extent.

The final pages of each book hide the best-kept secrets of the people of Israel. They are concealed within the strange lines drawn thereon. The man who will decipher these coded lines will bring peace to the entire world.

For a long time after The Hovering Being disappeared, I could not stop thinking about it. Is there any link between the being I saw and those old folk stories about other weird hovering beings? I am familiar with many strange names that can be attached to this being: Son of the Fire, The Great Spirit, The King of White Mice. Many peoples have prayed to this being but not us, the Sons of Israel, since we would never worship any holy men, hovering beings, or various ministers of God, for that matter. I'm absolutely sure that even if the Hovering Being would have been revealed in front of the 12 Tribes of Israel, they would have never prayed to it and worshiped it. The Jewish religion was and always will be the worshiping of one God. Therefore I would dare not to tell anyone about my strange encounter with the being. Occasionally it seems that I never actually met it and that my encounter with the being was nothing but a dream. All I have are these three books that bring evidence to my tantalizing meeting with it.

I will never forget this encounter on one of our holidays, the one that celebrates our arrival to the peace we so longed for at the Great Cave which is located at the Land of the Black Mountains with their sky-reaching peaks.

On that day we celebrated the first anniversary of our settling in the Great Cave. We had been traveling on an arduous journey from Persia and Madai[3] up until we arrived at the Land of the Black Mountains[4]. Twenty-three years had passed since the King of Evilness[5] had invaded our homeland, the land of Israel, and expelled us from it.

On that Holiday, I walked into my small alcove in the Great Cave where I used to write the Holy Books and I wrote a poem to honor our holiday:

People, my brothers,
We are not giving up!
But we shed a tear
Because we know that one day
Hope will shine again.

Enough! We shouted at the Evil
Enough! The human beast,
God, how could you
Create such evil?

When will the evil end
When will we return from exile?
Today I still am unable to rejoice
In the depths of the cave of liberty.

After writing the poem, I was very tired. My eyes slowly closed up and my head dropped forward onto the stone table. "Sssh … sssh …,"

---

[3] The Hebrew word for Iran of the Ancient World
[4] The Kashmir Region in India.
[5] The king of Assyria, Tiglath-Pilesar who expelled the ten lost tribes from the Land of Israel.

I heard a low quiet tone of a whistle behind me, like a hiss of a snake. It woke me up from my deep sleep. At first, I thought it was just a dream but the noise would not stop. I could hardly open my eyes but I turned around. In front of me, I saw a very strange image of a person that hovered and descended down to the floor of my room.

I rubbed my eyes in disbelief. A human being floating like an angel? I couldn't believe my eyes. *This is impossible!* I was terrified, *I'm in a nightmare!* I rubbed my eyes again and again but the being would not disappear.

"Angel," I said in a trembling voice, stormy pounding heart beating fast, fragile like a leaf. "Angel!" I implored, immersed with fear, and asking on my knees for mercy.

"Zvi Ben Yosef, I am neither an angel nor a God. I will not harm you. Stand on your feet!" the voice echoed in my head. I raised my head in surprise and looked at the being that stood in front of me. "I have no intention of harming you. Stand up!" the voice repeated in my head.

I suddenly noticed that its voice was not coming out of his mouth — the meaning of his words permeated my head but did not come through my ears.

The being approached me; placed a hand over my shoulder and commanded, "Stand up, man. Stand on your feet! Fear me not! Relax and hear my words." The touch of the being's hand on my shoulder transmitted strong waves of warmth through my entire body, and suddenly my fear vanished and was gone.

Having been released from my fear, I stood up and examined the strange being that stood in front of me and I demanded, "Who are you?! How can you hover like a bird?"

"Zvi Ben Yosef, listen to me! Remember my words. No one has ever heard these words. I come from a faraway planet. You cannot see this planet even if you had the most sophisticated devices! There is only one way to take a glimpse at these distant planets, by a special device called an Einiel[6]. It will take a very long time for humanity to see distant places like the Seven Worlds, such as my planet, by using this incredible device. The location of my home-world is the Triangle of Light. We have posted some space-stations for giving traffic-directions at some corners of the infinite cosmos. They are built of Einiel, and in the same manner as lighthouses, they are helpful in navigating the endless interplanetary universe.

"I arrived near Earth a long time before it was created. I had been investigating the solar system and the Milky Way, your planetary location. I witnessed how the sun exploded and the planets were created around it. I visited your planet at its nascent phase; I saw how life was formed. I witnessed the increase in the size of the first creatures that resulted – the humungous animals which are known as dinosaurs and others like them that used to step on the face of the earth. I watched them on their day of extinction. Obviously, I attested to the evolution of man on Earth, and I have a surprise for you – man was not created on planet Earth – man is a product of the Cosmos. Man does exist in so many forms on so many other planets. Your imagination can reach many beings that look like you. However, there are so many more that are differentiated from the human form, with which you're familiar. Some would be extremely intelligent and advanced; others, on other planets, would treat animals as though they were their own family members. These planets strive and prosper enormously; there is no hunger or poverty; no rich people either. Everyone has the same amount of assets. The lifespan of those human beings on other planets would last for thousands of years during which they would live in joy and happiness. There is an exclusive type of wealth that is known only to those cosmic human beings and it imparts on them the excellent learning which is needed for assembling new forms of highly-socially helpful products.

"However, intra-planetary journeys demand a huge amount of life-supporting systems to sustain life in space. There are hardly any human beings that can travel in space. I'm a being that closely resembles a human being but rather than being a human I'm a Robotan: an

---

[6] The eyes of God

immensely complex array of materials compose my body; I have a gigantic brain with a large working capacity, one which can be compared only to that of a thousand people. But I'm not an advanced version. Since I was built, some five billion years ago, there have been many more refined and advanced versions built. Every now and then some technical error can occur to me; I'd fix it very easily. In the event of a fatal non-repairable mechanical error, my service period as a Robotan would be terminated. The Interplanetary Control-Center will run a self-destruct protocol, and I will end up as a heap of ashes shortly afterward. There is no way for me to resist that since I'm only an emissary of the Control-Center.

"It was four thousand years ago when I visited Earth again. On that same day, I appeared in front of a big group of humans. My sight generated a tremendous storm of emotions and fears. The visage of my hovering image invoked many rites and worship. In many spots on Earth, human beings began to build many magnificent temples for worshiping me through strange religious rituals and ceremonies that glorified me as a being. You can obviously see that I am neither a God nor the son of a God; I'm only a Robotan and ever since my last appearance before men, I've tried not to appear again. I've visited planet Earth plenty of times and the number of rites has only kept increasing. I'm well aware of the impact of my visit on Earth and how it can potentially destroy the existing belief systems and create new ones. It will take many years until mankind will rid itself of these heathenish rites and ceremonies. The beings of the Triangle of Light have successfully built a computer that runs at very high speed, and we would race through our endless fascinating cosmos at this speed to observe the birth of new planets and death of old ones."

For a long time, the Son of the Planets transmitted his breathtaking and unperceivable story to me, and then, just in a wink of an eye, he disappeared into the ceiling of the cavern. For a long time, I was riveted to the spot, filled up with disbelief, digesting whether this was a true appearance; that it was not a dream that I dreamt. After long minutes of recovering from the spooky experience, I stood up and found three books lying on my table. I opened them and I realized that their pages were blank and unwritten. Lying next to them was a strange-looking quill, I used it to write the three books, in one consecutive writing line, never needing to dip the quill in ink. And thus, for many days I wrote the Story of the Son of the Planets. After completing them, I hid them in different hiding places within the cavern and didn't share my eminent secret with anybody else, from my fear to be laughed at or even being harmed by others. Perhaps when my final day comes I will share this monumental secret with my oldest son.

Friends and family members have been marveling about my behavior that appeared to be so atypical and they were trying to figure out what had suddenly happened to me. Now I'm telling the secret to you so that you could read and judge whether I am right.

The Book of the Son of the Planets

By Zvi Ben Yosef, the Scribe

Far away in the Great Space, in a place where even human imagination would find it hard to reach — this is where I live. My planet is located far from the reach of the human eye. It is in a place called the Triangle of Light. It is located in the Seventh Sky.

I am a very well-known being in your world. My name is inscribed in the hearts of many nations under many strange names. Many large tribes worship my image and pray to me — humans who wholeheartedly believe that I am either a God or an angel.

Since my appearance, nations and tribes have abandoned their religions and formed a new religion. I am the new God, the product of their hectic minds and beliefs, which are based on ignorance and backwardness.

I arrived here an infinite number of years ago before the Earth — where you are standing now — was created. I followed the birth of the sun with great interest. On the big fiery sun, I landed and examined it closely. The Mindneron, my spacecraft, and my body both were designed to withstand any temperature on the face of the sun and anywhere else.

Ever since my first landing there, I'd spent a long time on the sun on many visits, until one day, the spacecraft warned me of an impending eruption of stressful force from the bowels of the sun. I disregarded this warning and continued peacefully with my research.

The explosion was so strong that fragments of the sun reached far beyond the First Heaven.

These fragments flung like arrows all over the Seven Skies and became the meteorites and stars that you can see today in the sky. Personally, I wasn't damaged by the enormous explosion but the Mindneron was damaged, and ever since then, I have been unable to repair it and return to the Triangle of Light. It was a long time ago and I'm still waiting for my people to come and rescue me, but they are prevented from doing that because of that fickleness of mine that led me to ignore the warnings and to continue with my solar researches. And thus the Mindneron continues to float in this the First World unable to cross beyond it and travel to other worlds.

After the great explosion, parts of the power and memory systems of the Mindneron were lost. Neither made of steel nor from any other material which is known to mankind, the Mindneron will stay a mystery to mankind into the far future. It is made of a cosmic alloy, which cannot be found in your world, that can be inflated up like a balloon. However, it is a millionfold harder than any known material on Earth; a 100 cubic meter piece weighs like a gown that is worn by humans in the evening. Due to the wonders of another material, which is called Cosmobonim, the Mindneron is capable of speeds much higher than the speed of light. This speed enables us to move across immense distances and explore the vastness of the Seven Worlds.

The astronomical capacities we have to observe deep space will become known to future generations when they will have special flying telescopes, with the observational abilities that are limited to the First World. It will take thousands of years until human beings will learn how to utilize the Einiel capacity, which rather than being based on technological advancement can see beyond it. It will take tens of thousands of years until you, human beings, will learn to utilize those immense cosmic energies to produce cosmic materials that will replace your poor wearing-out bodies, which would be terminated shortly after your birth.

Being a highly sophisticated invention, the Mindneron, rather than being a simple familiar machine, is an immensely clever device which can perform an unbelievable number of tasks simultaneously and at an unimagined velocity. Theoretically, if we could join the entire brains of humans on Earth, it would still fall far behind the enormous brain capacity of one Mindneron. In the same way, it can solve the most complex mathematical problems; it can also read thoughts, raise questions, and give advice even on the most complicated problems.

And if you'd ask, what is the force setting the Mindneron in motion in its voyage between the worlds? Well, my friend, Zvi Ben Yosef, the source of this power is in the cosmos too. This enormous power is concentrated in a small cell at the center of the Mindneron. It is the size of an apple. This huge power is the Cosmos Liquid. Actually, it is not a liquid at all, but due to its remarkable flexibility, we call it a liquid. The Cosmos Liquid is produced in the Cosmos Sea. This sea has enormous currents and powerful waves.

Now I am going to tell you why I have returned to your world. Two Mindnerons went out of the Interplanetary Control-Center to rescue a Mindneron that was stuck in the great shell that encapsulates all of the Seven Worlds, which had been turned into a central object of research. You see, even we, with our gigantic capabilities, are facing some undecipherable challenges. The Interplanetary Control-Center had gotten a distress code, and we had to perform the rescue mission. With great efforts we rescued the staff of the Mindneron; however, the vessel was stuck.

In the framework of our journey across the Seven Worlds, we are investigating new methods of breaking through the great shell around them. One day and we will be able to break through the great shell and discover new things there, perhaps even the Gates of the Kingdom of Creation.

Now I am going to tell you about the tragic mistake that I had made — the mistake that caused me to wander around your world without being able to return to my planet. We managed to get to the Mindneron that was stuck in the shell around the worlds. With great effort, we rescued the two researchers who were trapped. As we completed this task, we headed back to the base. The two rescued researchers entered the leading Mindneron where the person in charge was sitting and I piloted the other Mindneron. On our way back, I suddenly noticed something strange on the surface of the sun. I quickly abandoned my Mindneron and landed on the sun to explore the strange event. A short time after I landed on the sun, there was an explosion and many fragments flew from it. The huge explosion damaged the Mindneron, greatly reducing its power. The Mindneron that I currently use does not have the capability of moving from one world to another.

When the person in charge saw the disaster, he immediately transmitted to me that my punishment would be to remain in this world for a long time. And this is how I am paying for my curiosity and irresponsibility.

Occasionally there are collisions between the Seven Worlds. These collisions lead to the eruption of cosmic lava that changes worlds. Your world keeps changing too. New planets are created and old ones disappear. The Seven Worlds continuously expand and shrink.

However, the main changes will occur millions of years from now, and then humans will live on the new planets. This is how the world goes. Old worlds fall apart and new ones are created. No world exists forever.

Lives that are very different from one another exist on the thousands of planets within the Seven Worlds. Your imagination cannot perceive how different these lives are from the lives of humans and how strange they are.

Your Bible says that the world was created in six days, six periods of creation. These were long periods in the development of life. It was only during the sixth and last period that humans like you appeared. I have already transmitted to you that the world in which you live, including the animals and plants, keeps changing. Thousands of years from now, there is going to be a change in the structure of the human body, so that humans will no longer appear as they do today.

The creation of your world has not yet been completed. New periods are about to come to your world. If the family of man does not unite in your tiny world, you will disappear. I can tell you something interesting that you cannot see right now. When the great sun exploded, many planets disappeared and new ones were created. Huge fires lit up your world. They could be seen from a huge distance. It was a beautiful sight. During this explosion, a planet was destroyed including all the interesting living creatures on it. This is how the worlds are — one world is created and another is destroyed.

Zvi Ben Yosef, I can read your mind and I can see that you find it hard to believe me. I know that my messages are strange and hard for the human brain to comprehend. But the day will come and the new human will come — the Man of the Worlds — who will be entirely different from the humans you know today. The Man of the Worlds will change the face of Earth.

Our planet has changed too, and so did our bodies. Our bodies have been rebuilt and have undergone many changes. And today, my friend, my body is immortal! We are no longer humans. We are rather members of the worlds, members of the cosmos. We are immortal.

"How can you possibly say that you are immortal? And how can humans rebuild their bodies?" I wondered with excitement.

Zvi Ben Yosef, your mind is filled with beliefs that have no basis. Humans are not going to understand what I say for many years. Many years will pass by until humans learn that the world is round like a ball and not flat like a dish. People will be executed by lunatics who say that the world is flat. Anybody who claims that it is round will be sentenced to death.

The planet Earth where you live is very much as my planet was in its beginning. These days, humans begin their first steps on Earth. Lightning, thunder, sun, moon, and other natural phenomena will fill the human being with fears. I must be cautious, with my appearance in front of people, which can become the basis for many strange beliefs? Later things will change, and humans will believe in people who claim that they have been sent on God's mission, but they will not bring peace to humans. I refer to these wild days as the Days of the Shell, since humans wrap themselves in many beliefs, just like a shell. These beliefs conceal the truth.

Humans will undergo tough times due to their strange beliefs. Many human beasts will appear in the world saying that they are messengers of the Creator of the worlds. These people will use their enormous power to steal, torture, and destroy anybody opposing them. No one will be able to overcome their power. Evil, ignorance, hostility, envy, stupidity, and war are the work of humans only.

Zvi Ben Yosef, now I am about to transmit to you information on what has happened on my planet? A long time before your world was destroyed and rebuilt; life had already existed on the planet that I come from. Our planet developed similarly to Earth where you live, but with some differences. Our planet went through nine periods of development. The first human, who looked very much like the humans currently living on Earth, appeared during the sixth period. We went through three more periods until the new type of human being had developed. We call this type the Hayboon. I am the descendent of the most advanced family of humans. I am a son of the Hayboons.

The actual change came after the Last War, which brought about the greatest change. The Last War was terrible, very cruel. It was completed quickly. Within a few moments of the time when war broke out on our planet, most of the inhabitants were killed. It took just a few seconds. The only survivors were the leaders of those nations, military commanders, and their family members, who were protected and ready to fight. Many scientists and their assistants survived as well. This was the final war on the planet where I come from.

Zvi Ben Yosef, you should know that many wars are about to take place in your small world as well. These wars will last for many years and there will be many casualties.

The Book of the Son of the Planets

The Last War

What can I tell you about that war? It was very short but it was a nightmare. The shock of the Last War was enormous. One disaster followed another. Upon the end of the Last War, the inhabitants of that planet changed totally. The very few survivors were united and there were no more enemies. This was the start of the great unification of the hostile rulers who were left without their nations.

A few days after the Last War, there were significant changes in the weather. The clouds were pouring rain of black mud, sand, stones, fish, and a huge amount of unidentifiable objects. The weather changed very quickly. Each day was different from the previous day. A very hot day turned into a cold stormy day.

Suddenly, something terrible appeared something that we had never experienced before. It started in a very strange manifestation. The inhabitants of the planet lost their balance. They walked as if they were floating. After many tests and studies, it became evident that the planet was losing its gravity. The news shocked the remaining survivors.

The new disaster kept getting worse. First, the inhabitants of the planet started to wear heavy belts stuffed with lead around their waist. They wrapped belts around their sheep and all domestic animals. They kept adding more and more weight to their bodies every day until it was impossible to add any more. One disaster followed another; bad news kept coming in every day. The sea, ponds, rivers, and all sources of water started evaporating very quickly, and the soil was dry as a desert. The clouds no longer produced any rain. Large clouds of dust went up with the blowing winds until they slowly disappeared into the sky. Tiny animals and insects floated in the clouds of dust until they too disappeared into the gray skies.

The planet's inhabitants were very scared when they saw what was going on. They were afraid that, without water, animals, and insects, there would no longer be any life on the planet.

Several days later, something else developed. The planet's inhabitants felt a huge pull toward the sunlight, which was becoming increasingly weaker amidst the clouds of dust. They started feeling that their bodies no longer needed food and water. All they wanted was to have some sunlight.

"Why aren't we hungry anymore? Aren't we going to die of hunger?" the planet's inhabitants asked fearfully.

Strange and unexplained changes occurred in the plants too. Trees and all kinds of plants turned soft and flexible like rubber. Every mild wind made the trees move and bend to the ground. It was very weird to see a tall, thick tree moving around as if drunk or treetops hitting the ground. A few days later, the roots of trees were climbing up out of the ground, extending a long way upwards. The planet's inhabitants were surprised by the changes. They watched the trees that were moving about very slowly, making sounds like drums in the middle of the forest.

They then realized that the trees had drastically changed, turning into something that looked very much like ... a human body. When a branch was broken or a tree was uprooted, a scream was heard and a reddish liquid resembling blood came out of the trunk of the trees. The planet's scientists were astounded, witnessing the massive destruction and changes. "We don't have much time left to live on this planet. The situation is almost hopeless," they said as they embarked on one final effort to save the dying planet.

After extensive testing, the planet's scientists reached the conclusion that, within one year, human bodies would change into plants. The scientists did not want anybody to know about their terrible revelation. People would go out of their minds if they knew about it, the scientists determined, and so they vowed not to tell their secret to anybody. From that moment on, they tried even harder to find a solution to the coming calamity.

After many months of hard work, the scientists stopped their research. They were desperate. And then, when it seemed that there was no hope, an amazing discovery changed their attitude. They figured that gravity was going to completely disappear three days before the end of the year. Once the scientists arrived at this conclusion, they understood the solution to the coming calamity. They were unanimous in their resolve … they had to move the planet, and the best time to do so would be exactly when gravity completely disappeared. Additional testing and research confirmed that this imaginative option was the only one left, despite all the dangers involved.

Moving the planet to another location was the scientists' greatest challenge. They started accumulating all the sources of energy that were left on the planet. They kept these sources in an underground area. After a short time, they built a very large launching installation. They then gathered the planet's remaining inhabitants, preparing them for the great day. The plan to move the whole planet from its location and fly it into space scared the planet's inhabitants. For many months, they kept arguing with one another. The majority of inhabitants eventually decided that this irrational plan had no chance. They continued to covet sunlight and refused to worry. These uninformed clowns ridiculed the plan of flying the planet into space. None of them knew the terrible secret.

About one month before the end of the year, more amazing things occurred. Large stones and giant rocks were torn off. They started floating and going up to the sky as if they were birds. Trees were moving faster looking for underground sources of water. During the dark nights, the trees galloped rapidly as if they were ghosts. They made sounds like those of humans crying and screaming. Large forests were seen wandering, fighting against smaller forests that had found some water. All the small bushes and trees disappeared. Only trees with thick trunks survived, and they were fighting one another fiercely. Many times, trees torn from their place in this terrible war, went up to the sky, screaming loudly. Roots of trees were seen making their way around as if blind. They were shivering due to the lack of water, crying like babies. Many of the planet's inhabitants shed tears when they saw these dreadful sights.

Twenty days before the end of the year, water in the sea started evaporating at an amazing speed. Fish went up with the water — both tiny and giant fish rose up and disappeared into the sky. Animals who no longer had any shelter or hideouts went up and disappeared into space.

Ten days later, the inhabitants could no longer recognize their planet. The change was enormous. All lakes and seas were totally dried up; all animals, cattle, sheep, and insects had disappeared. Most of the plants and trees disappeared too. Tall mountains turned into valleys.

From their large shelter, the inhabitants watched terrible things happen right before their eyes. They saw their bodies going through sudden changes. Their bodies started to shrink, their skins became dry, their hair started falling out, and their hearts almost stopped beating. All laws of nature changed. When the planet's inhabitants saw the total devastation, they felt desperate. Their sense of despair was so deep that a number of people left the main shelter and quickly disappeared into the sky, screaming.

Scientists, seeing the disaster taking place right before their eyes, unanimously decided to carry out their plan of moving the planet without waiting for permission from the remaining inhabitants. Three hours before the great experiment, the bodies of elderly inhabitants started to grow branches. Their legs started growing tiny roots. Many grew scared. They leaped from the shelter into space.

Three hours later, as the huge burners were ignited; the planet's inhabitants felt a powerful turbulence that made the entire planet shake. A few moments later they heard very loud thunder as if the world was about to fall apart. All of that took place for only a fraction of a second, and suddenly the planet took off upwards, its speed increasing with each second. After a few minutes of fear and tension, the inhabitants understood that their whole planet was on its way into space. About an hour after takeoff, they started feeling that their belts were heavy again. "Gravity is returning!" they shouted happily. But their joy was even greater when they realized that all the changes that had previously occurred stopped instantly.

The planet continued through space for twenty years until it reached its destination — the region of the Triangle of Light. Many of the inhabitants died during their long voyage in space; only a few of them managed to survive until the end of the voyage. No one was happy when they reached the Triangle of Light. Their fear of the future was immense. The few trees that survived stopped their wandering about, but they remained flexible and the sound of their cry was heard all over the great deserted plains.

A few years later, new changes started appearing in the humans' bodies. First, the human heart stopped functioning, and later all the inner organs deteriorated. But the strangest change of all was the new growth. The planet's inhabitants were surprised to find that their bodies quickly grew new organs to replace the old ones. Within a short time, almost nothing resembling humans was left. What had existed before the Last War broke out was no longer there. Now you can understand why we are so different from humans living on Earth. The life of a new human in the Triangle of Light region was greatly extended to the point that the planet's inhabitants lived for tens of thousands of years. Women changed too. Their hair started growing again, but they were unable to give birth. "Without giving birth, we will no longer exist," the inhabitants said. They started searching for a solution to their new problem.

After about twenty-five thousand years of research, the scientists of the planet succeeded in realizing the great dream of humanity: eternal life. This new revolution changed the face of the planet. Man's fear of death vanished. More changes occurred in the human body. The sex organs disappeared — there were no longer any differences between men and women. Now that their fears had vanished, the inhabitants were highly motivated to start researching and learning about the world around them.

Zvi Ben Yosef, I see that you don't believe I am immortal. Indeed, there are times when my body goes into hibernation for a period of renewal. When I wake up, a new body appears. Whenever our bodies deteriorate or are destroyed, we go into hibernation to replace our bodies with new ones. In fact, our body is changed but our central charger does not change. Each time that our bodies are in hibernation, we move our charger to the place called the Control-Center, where we store our charge until the renewal process ends. In this way, we continue to be immortal.

The inhabitants of my planet made great achievements in their long-term studies. They made great discoveries. These discoveries and inventions brought us closer to the secrets of Creation. But the limits of creation cannot be reached! And even if we make very big steps, we still have a long road ahead of us to discover the tiniest parts of this secret.

Now that our planet is located in the Triangle of Light, it provides us with all our needs.

"What? You never die?" I said in amazement. "There are no births, no deaths, no food, no life … how is this possible?" I kept repeating.

Zvi Ben Yosef, you are unable to comprehend this. Man's brain is tiny and very limited. Tens of thousands of years are going to pass by until it gains insight about this word which is called *Life*.

I'm the Robotan who has been traveling through planets for billions of years, can see everything; I'm an infinite treasure of knowledge and understanding. Notwithstanding, I keep on learning many new things about the outer shell which is encapsulating our Seven Skies. Do I live? Well my friends, the scribe, I'm living to my maximal capacity! Life has not been given as a privileged thing exclusively for mankind! So, at the same time, I ache for the injustice and stupidity of other worlds and of their despotic, immoral, insensitive rulers! Yes, it's true that I don't feel any physical pain but my conscience is bleeding in the face of such cruelty of those human beasts whose hunger for power and wealth will never end.

I am confirming that everything written here is true.

Zvi Ben Yosef, the author.

As Sue finished reading the translation, she closed her eyes and whispered, "Now I understand the professor's words. It is impossible to publish this diary without having evidence beyond any reasonable doubt."

"How did the diary get into the stranger's hands? Are we going to meet the mysterious stranger again? Sue, what do you think? Should we tell Dad about the amazing event that happened to us?" I could not stop talking out of excitement.

Sue kept quiet for a long time. She lay down on the armchair and looked at the translation of the diary, again and again, saying nothing.

Chapter 6

A Surprising Visit

The following day, we went on an inspiring tour of Jerusalem's mixture of ancient glory and modern western culture. At the Wailing Wall, the only remaining part of the ancient Jewish Temple, we watched in awe as masses of worshippers that were loudly reciting their prayers. We returned to our hotel at sundown and were happy to see Dad waiting for us at the reception hall.

"I see that this time you weren't thrown out of this hotel," Dad said humorously. "Please take a shower, change your clothes, and let's have supper together."

"Dan, are you going to tell Dad the rest of the story?" asked Sue as we returned to our rooms.

"I don't think so. Dad is not going to believe us and he will probably think that we are a little off the wall."

During our meal, we talked about our visit to Jerusalem and the interesting places that we had seen, but we said nothing about our great adventure.

"I am glad to hear that your tour in the city wasn't boring. Now, what do you think about staying here for another week? I have to complete something very important. You'll be able to use the services of the tourism company the hotel recommends for trips around the country."

"Dad, you really shouldn't worry about us. This country is really very interesting, and we'll be happy to take a tour," I said enthusiastically.

"Oh, I am really glad to hear that. You really are an A-Team," Dad said with an amused look in his eyes.

Hmmm, interesting…what is going on in the old man's mind? I wondered when I saw the look in his eyes and his famous unrevealing smile.

The following day, after saying goodbye to Dad, we went to a travel agency that was not far from the hotel where we were staying.

"Yes, we can definitely recommend tours to a few great places in Israel," said a young, elegantly but pompously dressed travel agent. "I would recommend going to the Judean Desert and the Dead Sea, which is the lowest point in the world, where you can both float on the water and read a newspaper. You can also visit one of the best-known sites in the history of the Jewish nation, Masada. Tomorrow morning at 7:00 a.m. an air-conditioned minibus tour is leaving from this location and you are invited to join it."

"Sounds good," Sue said.

"It really does," I agreed, and we reserved our seats.

The next morning, punctually at 7:00 a.m., we sat in the air-conditioned minibus on our way to an unknown land. "Dan, did you manage to understand anything of those strange designs drawn in the diary?" Sue asked me shortly after our bus left Jerusalem. "Is it possible that the Son of the Planets is still exploring our planet?"

"Sue, as soon as we return from our tour, we are going to look for Mr. D'Acosta. I have a strange feeling that our friend continues to wander around the Old City looking for something that we aren't aware of yet."

I believed that the trip to the Dead Sea would be devoted to entertainment and rest, but I quickly discovered how my wishful thinking was wrong. We passed through the enchanted streets of Jerusalem and then headed down the southern mountain slopes toward the Judean Desert. As we left Jerusalem, the green-colored scenery vanished as if by magic. The oaks and Judas trees disappeared and were replaced by miserable-looking desert bushes and brown rocks.

The minibus raced along the black asphalt road through the arid canyons of the desert and descended towards the lowest point in the world. It didn't take long until we arrived at the road leading to Jericho. We turned right, and all of a sudden the Dead Sea emerged magnificently tranquil and still. A marvelous bath of salt, I pondered. This sea and the sulfur springs flowing into it there are known for their healing qualities, as they work magic on people suffering from skin conditions.

We disembarked with our tour on a wide-open beach and joined the many bathing visitors. Indeed my body began to float in it as if I was a wooden beam. Shortly after we bathed and enjoyed the magic of the Dead Sea we continued on to Masada. The road along the Dead Sea is surrounded by large stone mountains and the biting winds of the desert had eroded them and formed them in the shape of ancient-looking monsters. Amongst them I noticed in that primordial landscape the stone pillar known as Lot's Wife that sits silently and motionlessly, staring at the baking desert.

As we approached our next destination, the driver started, "Attention, please. We are about to arrive at the well-known fortress of Masada, a symbol of the Jewish nation's heroism in the fight against foreign invaders. Here, in this place, a small group of fighters stood against the large and strong Roman legions and fought against them desperately. About nine hundred men, women, and children held off the Roman war machine for seven months, but when they eventually realized that no hope was left, they decided to die as heroes rather than see their children and wives taken prisoners and sold as slaves. After some raging and tough battles, the Roman legions entered Masada, and could not believe their eyes. The fighters and their families were scattered dead all over the area. They all had taken their own lives."

A cable car took us very slowly to the top of the flat summit. Throughout our ascent, we surveyed the desert landscape, which probably hadn't changed a lot since the suicidal death of those ancient warriors. Once on the summit, we surveyed the incredible views. Down below me I could see the ramparts the Romans built to blockade the besieged rebels ... and in my mind's eye, I pictured the struggle for life and death, their battle cries; the triumphant yells of the invaders that storm into Masada ... and the bloodcurdling silence that welcomed them and the streams of blood.

The sight of a familiar-looking image that suddenly appeared down below, brought my daydreaming to a sudden end. To look more closely I turned to a man who was using the tourist authority's stationary binoculars not far from where we stood, and asked, "Sir, would you please let me have a quick glance? I have a friend whom we became separated from and I suffer from myopia".

The man stepped aside saying, "Please sir, it's my great pleasure."

I thanked him and moved behind the binoculars to survey the surface where I noticed that blurred image had been. I saw Arthur D'Acosta standing in the company of other tourists next to a restaurant.

"Sir, how could I ever thank you?" I said briefly, grasped Sue's hand in mine, and began to walk quickly in the direction of the cable cars.

"Dan, what's going on?!"

"Sue, don't waste time on chattering. I just saw Mr. D'Acosta down below next to a restaurant in the company of other tourists. We must not miss our chance to meet with him."

We got on the next cable car, pushed our way on, and descended to the desert floor. Exiting the car, I spotted Mr. D'Acosta near the big restaurant, walking in the company of his large group of associates.

My energies were renewed as I hurried to close the distance between us, waving to him and calling his name with excitement, "Hello, Mr. D'Acosta!" I was baffled when he just turned and walked away as if we had never met.

I stopped in sheer amazement. *What's wrong? Why was he ignoring me? Why? There must be some logical explanation for that, but what can I do now?*

After a while, his group moved inside to sit at one of the bigger tables. Purposefully, we sat at a table next to him and ordered two coffees and pastries. I guessed Sue was flabbergasted by this awkward event but she didn't utter a word. She sat as if she was part of a theatre audience.

Could my identification of him be mistaken? Now we could closely examine the face of the evasive stranger. After watching him for a while, we reached the conclusion that indeed it was him. The small scar above his eye, the result of his struggle with the robbers, could be seen very clearly. It was definitely Mr. D'Acosta.

Sue finally said, "Dan, this is the person we are looking for. Yet he is clearly trying to avoid us".

"What can I do?" I uttered with disappointment. "D'Acosta doesn't want to talk to us and he is openly ignoring us. The elusive fish," I whispered to Sue. "He ought to give us some explanations."

After eating, the group left the restaurant and went to the nearby hostel. We followed them. At the entrance, we asked the receptionist to tell us where our friend Mr. Arthur D'Acosta was staying.

The receptionist looked through his guest list and said, "I am sorry. We don't have a guest by this name."

"Can you please check again?" Sue asked politely.

Looking impatient, the receptionist checked the list again, said "Sorry," and returned to his duties.

We waited until the receptionist left his desk for a moment and then we went through the hallway, knocking on every door in our search for the stranger. We checked all the rooms without result. Mr. D'Acosta had just vanished. We had seen our slippery friend entering the hostel, and there was no exit other than the main entrance. I felt embarrassed and confused. Tired and disappointed, we went back to the cable car and our group of tourists. When we got near the cable car, I looked up and saw the door closing. And then I saw those smiling, familiar eyes again. I froze in place for a moment. D'Acosta, the slippery eel, was in the car!

We stood impatiently in the long line waiting for the next car. After a wait that seemed like an eternity, we rode back up to Masada. As soon as we reached the ancient guard room where the car discharges its passengers, we resumed our search.

Walking softly with small steps, I made my way throughout Masada, looking carefully, with Sue following me. We saw many people but the stranger was not among them. I walked toward the southern part of the fortress and then completed a full circle around Masada. But D'Acosta's disappearance was like the morning dew.

Could it be that our slippery friend was already on his way down? I rushed to the guard room with its view of the descending cable cars but found nothing. I was covered with sweat and wiped it away angrily. We continued feeling a mess, our noses out of joint, moving in a circular motion around Masada. The group of tourists with whom we had arrived passed by us.

"Why don't you join the tour?" the guide asked. I apologized and told him that I was looking for a friend. I described the looks of Mr. D'Acosta.

"Oh, really?" one of the women announced in a creaky voice. "Just a few minutes ago I saw a man looking very much like the person you have described. He was heading along the narrow path towards the large water pits, to the left of the northern palace."

"Thank you so-so much"

"By the way", she added and smiled, "your friend is a very good-looking man,"

Before she could finish speaking I was pacing hurriedly toward the water cisterns on the western side of Masada.

"Dan, please slow down! I cannot keep up with you!" I heard Sue's voice but I couldn't overcome my intense desire to find Mr. D'Acosta, not even for a second.

Chapter 7

The Fall

I quickly arrived at the first water pit. Without any hesitation, I went down the stairs.

After a few steps down, I stopped and waited for Sue. It was very dark inside the cave. I couldn't see anything. "Don't be afraid. Go down the stairs very slowly," I said to her.

"Dan, where do you want to go down to? The cistern is dark. I can't see anything."

"You're right, we should get a flashlight. Sue, maybe you can get off Masada quickly and get a flashlight or a candle. I will wait here on the path leading toward the water pits."

After a long time, Sue finally returned, holding candles and matches in her hands. "I am sorry. I couldn't find a flashlight anywhere," she said.

"This is good enough. I am going down into the pit. Are you coming with me?"

"I really don't know. I don't believe that Mr. D'Acosta is hiding in the pits. It doesn't make sense to me."

"It is worth checking anyway. I will proceed slowly and you'll follow me."

I held Sue's hand and we carefully went down the stairs to the pit, all the way down to its bottom. I lit up a candle and continued to walk very carefully while Sue followed me closely.

To be honest, I also had fears about the unknown, but I tried to display courage. The candlelight cast shadows that looked like they were dancing on the wall. Suddenly I felt the ground being dropped from under my feet. We were falling … down, down … a thought flashed through my mind … *we were* falling!

Circles of lights in vibrant colors were flashing in front of my eyes when I slowly opened them. "What is it? Where am I?" I whispered. My eyes adjusted to the light. I was in the center of a large room painted in white, lying on a white bed. "What's going on here?" I demanded loudly,

I noticed I was connected to a transparent bag of fluid by an IV tube that was attached to my hand. "Is this a hospital? It's impossible!" I demanded to know.

The door opened, and a nurse entered the room. She flashed a wide smile to me and said happily, "Great! I am glad to see that you have regained consciousness."

"Where is Sue? What has happened to her?"

"You must be talking about the young lady who was found with you. Don't worry. Her condition is quite good, just a few bruises. You can see her in the next room as soon as you feel better."

"How did I get here?" I asked. All at once, the memory of our tour to Masada and the descent into the water cistern came back to me. "Nurse! Who brought me here?"

"You were found at the foot of the Snake Path, both of you had fainted. You probably fell down when you were going down the path."

"I fell down?" I was angry. "No way! How could I fall down in a place I never been to before? Rather, I …" I immediately stopped talking. *I shouldn't tell anyone what had happened. No one is going to believe me anyway, not if I say I fell inside a water pit. They might refuse to release me, claiming I have a concussion and must stay in the head trauma ward.*

"If you wish, I can read to you the description that we have received from the nice man who found you at the foot of the Snake Path. You would probably like to thank him," the nurse said and left the room. A moment later, she returned holding a notebook from which she read the following details:

At 2:00 p.m., while walking at the foot of Masada, I saw a couple, a boy and a girl, lying unconscious at the foot of the Snake Path. I assume that they stumbled on their way up the Snake Path. In my humble opinion, it should be made clear to them that they should not attempt to do any climbing in places that are unfamiliar to them. Not all places are reachable.

(signed) Arthur D'Acosta

"What?" I said angrily but immediately stopped myself again. I felt a terrible pain penetrating my head, making my vision blurry. *I don't believe it! This slippery bastard is just laughing at me. I am going to go back and dig through all the water pits until I find where he is hiding.*

"Did he give his address?" I innocently asked the nurse. "We would like to thank him."

"No," the nurse answered. "I am sorry. Only his name is on the record."

After a long rest, I left my bed and after a short quest for Sue, I found her.

"I told you so!" were the first words that she said. "We are lucky that they found us so quickly. We could have still been in the cistern, and who knows what would have happened to us then?"

"I have a surprise for you. The place where they found us was not the pit but at the foot of the Snake Path."

"What? Which path? What are you talking about?"

"Mr. D'Acosta himself brought us here. He reported that he had found us at the foot of the Snake Path. It is all written in the hospital's report. The nurse read it to me."

"There is something very strange here," Sue whispered in amazement.

I could not argue with her.

I will never forget the examinations that I underwent from all the medical students in the hospital. They were like bees busily buzzing around me, taking my blood from all locations, taking my temperature at any occasion, examining my pupils, and taking x-ray photographs of each and every bone I have. Three days later, just as I felt that my patience was about to reach its limits, I received a discharged letter from the hospital and said farewell to the flock of students who could not conceal their disappointment. Throughout the period I was there, I had a strange feeling that should I had stayed any longer with all these medical examinations I might end up in a jug of formaldehyde in a preserved condition. When we finally were outside the hospital, I took Sue's hand in mine and we hurried to get as quickly as possible away from the gate of the hospital and back to our hotel in Jerusalem.

"Sue," I said, "I think we should call the professor and tell him the news."

"I don't think he is going to be interested, but there is nothing to lose. Let's get his opinion on this new development."

I called Professor Alon. After a few polite words, I told him briefly about my visit to Masada and about how we ended it at the hospital after a fall.

"What fall? What are you talking about?"

"Thanks to our friend, Mr. D'Acosta, who supposedly found us at the foot of the Snake Path and brought us to the hospital."

The professor laughed quietly. "Well, my young friend! I am really glad to hear that you were not seriously hurt after falling into a dire abyss. I wish you a quick recovery. I have a lot of work to do. We'll talk later. Goodbye and see you soon."

He hung up. I held the phone receiver for a long time, annoyed at his reaction. His sarcastic words, "I am really glad to hear that you were not seriously hurt after falling into a dire abyss," echoed in my mind.

"The professor does not believe my story!" I told Sue with great disappointment.

"That is obvious! It is impossible to stay alive after that kind of fall. The professor is wishing you a quick recovery from all of your weird stories," she laughed.

"Sue, be serious. How did Mr. D'Acosta manage to drag us all the way from the water cistern and then down and out of Masada, and at the same time stay unnoticed by the hundreds of other visitors? What did he mean in the hospital report that 'not all places are reachable'? Was he trying to tell us that we are unable to reach him? We should return and examine the place very thoroughly."

To my surprise, Sue agreed without any hesitation.

The following day we obtained ropes for climbing, a small hammer, and two powerful flashlights. Now we were equipped with all the tools necessary to search inside the dark cistern. The day after that we were back at Masada. Immediately we looked for the way leading to the Snake Path and shortly afterward we were there. I looked around for a few moments, peering at the huge rock that rose into the sky above our heads.

"I'm confused," I said. "I don't see any path leading from the water cisterns in the west toward the Snake Path in the south."

"Maybe there is a hidden tunnel," Sue said. We searched with our eyes for a hidden opening in the huge rock, but could not see any.

"We have no choice," I told Sue. "We have to go back to the top of Masada and check the water pit where we fell." We headed for the cable car.

About thirty minutes later we were standing at the cistern opening waiting for the tourists to leave.

"Sue, I have a plan. I am going to tie myself with the rope while you stand on the bottom step and light up my way. If I fall, the rope will catch me and you'll be able to call for help."

"Dan, I am afraid that going down into the cistern alone is not a good idea."

"That's true, but if we want to learn the truth about our fall, and what Mr. D'Acosta was doing inside the water cistern? We better descend together and carefully."

I started to step down at a slow pace while Sue followed me to the last step. I hammered two spikes into the wall of the water cistern and tied one end of the rope to them with the other end tied around my waist. Moving slowly with small steps I reached the point at which we had fallen the previous time.

A few steps later I stopped, took a folding hoe out of my backpack, and started to dig cautiously. The soil was soft and I had no difficulty digging. All kinds of wild thoughts started to race through my mind: *Perhaps there are secret passages that will be revealed only after pushing a secret button that may open a hidden door? Or perhaps a magical phrase like that in the story of Ali Baba and the Forty Thieves which will open a secret door?*

After spending a long time searching and digging in the floor of the cistern, I felt very tired. I stopped and called to Sue, "There is neither an abyss nor a hidden cave or revolving doors in here; absolutely nothing. Perhaps we didn't fall on the Snake Path? Maybe it was only an illusion."

"I'm quite sure that we fell into a hole. I remember the feeling of falling," she answered.

"But you can see that there is no sign of or any secret openings or holes."

"Dan, right now it is late and I am very hungry. Let's go to the hostel, and tomorrow morning we'll continue our search."

We made our way to the hostel, hungry and disappointed. After a cold shower, I had new ideas. *Perhaps we must find some secret covered room in the cistern. I don't need to do excavation; hitting on few spots with a hammer might be enough. A hollow, hidden, and covert place behind the wall will echo back.* I recalled from my memory everything I knew from detective movies.

This could be the solution! I should look for an echo. I tried to tell Sue about my new idea but she had already fallen asleep. I would have to keep my new revelation to myself until morning.

The alarm clock awoke us at 7:00 a.m. First, we quickly reorganized our equipment. Then we took the first cable car to the top of Masada. Again we found ourselves climbing down onto the cistern floor. I fastened the rope to the spikes that were still in place from the day before and tied a rope to my body once more. I took the hammer out of my bag and began hitting the floor vigorously. "Masada, tell me your secret," I whispered to the walls around me.

I hit the floor tirelessly for a long time, then switched to the walls. I had a strange feeling that I was being watched all the time and heard obscure sounds while I was banging the walls with the hammer. Fear began to creep into my heart and I lit the walls all the way around with my flashlight but couldn't see anything.

The hard work left me too exhausted to stand. I sunk down to take a rest, took the water bottle, and drank all the water in it. "The hell with this place!" I said angrily and threw the bottle away.

I heard the sound of steps approaching from behind me and was scared to death.

"Dan, my young and obstinate friend, stand up please, and follow me. Young lady, you are invited too," the voice called out to Sue. "Follow me. You have nothing to worry about."

Sue came down following the rope. I untied the rope from my waist and led Sue by the hand onward.

Chapter 8

On the Verge of the Secret

"Are you ready to follow me?" Mr. D'Acosta asked very earnestly. "Don't rush to say yes. You won't be able to change your mind later on, and you'll not be able to go back."

I did not understand the import of Mr. D'Acosta's words, but I agreed to follow him without any hesitation, as did Sue.

Mr. D'Acosta took two handkerchiefs out of his pocket, covered our eyes, quietly took our hands, and asked us to follow him. He then stopped and released his grip from our hands. I stood, tense and nervous, waiting, and wondering what my friend would do next. Then I felt Mr. D'Acosta's hands removing the handkerchief from my eyes.

The bright colors of daylight, with its bluish tints, dazzled me.

"What's that?" I asked, surprised. "Where am I?"

I saw a large room, in the center of which stood a large, wooden table and six chairs. A large bed covered with white clean linens was in the corner of the room.

Mr. D'Acosta smiled and said, "Come on, let me show you around."

We found ourselves in a large house with three furnished rooms, which looked much like the rooms in my own family's house. There was a kitchenette, a bathroom with a shower, and various household objects. But something strange caught my attention. There were no windows, but even so, the house was brightly lit up. And where was this strange light coming from? I looked in vain around for the source of light. No windows, no lamps. Was I dreaming? I rubbed my eyes, but the picture vividly stayed in front of my eyes.

At the end of the brief tour, we went back to the room where we had started and sat around the table. Mr. D'Acosta left the room and returned holding a wooden tray with three cups of hot fragrant tea.

We had never before gulped our tea so fast. We were eager to start with our questions.

Mr. D'Acosta raised his hand, smiling from ear to ear. "Well, I see you have many questions, but before I start answering, you should receive a gift." He took a tiny box out of his pocket, opened it very carefully, and removed two black rings from the box.

"What?" I called out. "Are you going to marry us?"

"Dear Dan, both of you are going to marry my secrets, and this ring will make sure that you don't disclose the things you are going to hear or see in this place to anyone. This ring will keep your lips sealed."

When Mr. D'Acosta uttered those words, a strange spark passed through his eyes. His gaze made it clear that the man wasn't kidding. With a shaking hand, I took the black ring and examined it intently.

"I am warning you again that, from the moment you wear these rings, you will not be allowed to tell my secrets to anybody ... the moment you open your mouths to tell my secrets, you are going to die! Look at the ring. If you have any doubts about maintaining this secret I will erase the memory of our meeting from your brain and send you away. Well, my young friends, the moment of truth has come. Can you undertake such a strong commitment?"

"Yes, definitely!" we answered in unison. "Please tell us your big secret."

As I placed the ring on my right hand, I felt a warm wave of heat flushing through my body. The grip of the ring on my finger became tighter. I tried to remove it ... but couldn't. I realized that the ring would stay on my finger forever.

"Well my friends, first of all, you should know that both of the rings that protect my secrets were made hundreds of years ago, and people will learn about their powers only many years from now. This ring can read all of your thoughts from this moment until your last day alive."

Mr. D'Acosta sipped from the hot tea and told us his unbelievable story. "As you know, my name is Arthur D'Acosta. I come from a well-known family from the city of Cordoba in Spain. My family's ancestral roots hail from nobility and many of the family members held top-ranked positions in the leadership of the country and the Church. When I was thirteen years of age, I participated in a strange ceremony in one of the rooms at the estate. Since that day, I was no longer that mischievous happy youth that was loved by his friends. The transformation was enormous."

Chapter 9

Descendent of Marranos

D'Acosta took a deep breath and continued with his story:

"Nothing could have prepared me for such a special event as the one that occurred when I had my birthday at the age of thirteen. One day, during the early evening hours, my family members and a few close friends were gathered in my father's study. Everybody congratulated and embraced me, and bestowed many gifts on me. At first, I didn't understand, but slowly everything became clearer.

"My father was standing in the center of the room. He took two black leather-covered boxes with black leather straps out of a cloth bag. He placed one of the boxes on my forehead and the other one on my left arm, and he wrapped the long leather strap around my arm seven times. My father then opened an ancient book and started to read from it, in a language that I had never before heard. Occasionally the guests would join in, whispering a few words together. When my father was done reading, he placed the book in front of me and instructed me to repeat his words verbatim. I did as I was told, but I didn't understand any of the words that I said."

"When it was over I asked my father, 'What is this strange ritual about?'

" 'Son,' my father began, 'there is a deep secret we have been keeping in our family for hundreds of years. Now that you have reached the age of thirteen, you are considered an adult, a member of the Jewish nation who is undertaking the obligation to do the *mitzvoth*[7]. My dear son, the time has come to make you aware that our entire family and all our friends in this room are Marranos.'

" 'What?' I yelled with disbelief. I was about to collapse. 'This … no, no, that's impossible!' I resisted.

"My father calmed me down. I lowered my voice and felt my pent-up rage surging in me. Then I uttered, 'No! This is impossible. We are not a Marrano family. Our uncle is a strict observing Catholic bishop, and we attend church every Sunday!'

" 'Yes, son. We all attend church. The good ones; the bad ones; the crooks; the thieves; and we are like everybody else,' my father said, with a bitter chuckle.

"Other participants sadly smiled in response to my angry words.

" 'Son,' my uncle, the bishop, turned to me and said, 'as a matter of fact those who gave us this derogatory name were Marranos themselves. We are descendants of the people who gave the world the belief in monotheism. Jesus and his Apostles too were members of the Jewish people. Thousands of years ago, when many of the world's nations were heathens and cannibals, the Jewish people had already held the basis of this world, The Ten Commandments.

" 'You've most probably learned about *Innocentius* who was known by his nickname, *The Animal*. This maddened person forced many of our people to convert to Christianity by using harsh torture. Thus for example in 1391 A.D. an incited mob racked our people, a community that had lived in Spain for hundreds of years, burnt them alive in their homes. The remnants were forced to convert.'

---

[7] Mitzvoth = commandments of the Jewish Law

"It took me a long time to gather my wits again. My confusion and denial were replaced by a strong passion to know who I was — who my people are. These questions and many more others echoed in my head for long after the event with those small black leather boxes containing scrolls of parchment inscribed with verses from the Torah called *tefillin*. For many days I gathered information about the survival of my people despite thousands of years of exile, humiliation, persecution, and suffering. Step by step, I learned the history of my people, which began around four thousand years ago.

"I did not leave my room for many days. My old friends kept away from me and I was no longer interested in being with them. All I wanted was to learn as much as possible about the history of my people. One issue especially bothered me. That was the destiny of the ten tribes who were expelled by the Assyrian king following the fall of the city of Samaria, around the year 700 BC, and since then have been lost. I was intrigued by the thorny question of where they were expelled to and where they can be found today. From a large nation of the Twelve Tribes, only two had survived.

"The mystery had kept on bothering me without giving me any rest. For many years I continued to search and obtained knowledge about the ten lost tribes. A vast source of interesting information I found in the Hebrew University in Jerusalem as well as in a very interesting book on the *Rambam*, a Jewish philosopher and physician who lived in my town of Cordoba about eight hundred years ago. This philosopher too was forced to flee Spain out of fear of the anti-Semitic persecutions. I was taken by the wisdom of the Rambam's books that encouraged me to continue my searches for the glorious roots of the Jewish nation.

"One of the things I read there which impressed me a lot was the *Epistle-Yemen,* letters sent by the Rambam to the Jews who were persecuted and humiliated in Islamic countries. For a long time, I couldn't fall asleep after reading these terrible letters and realizing to what extent my people, the Jews, were persecuted and humiliated wherever they went.

"One day I found a thin book and after I read it my life was changed and I embarked on a long and difficult journey in my search after the lost ten tribes. This thin book told of Jewish settlements that had been discovered in remote places in the world. These people could possibly be the descendants of the ten lost tribes. One interesting story mentioned a large Jewish settlement called Derbent near the Caspian Sea in Dagestan[8]. The inhabitants of this place spoke the *Tat* language and were called *Tetim,* and lived at the foot of a mountain called *Dagh Chufuty,* which means 'Mountain of the Highland Jews'. However, the strangest and most amazing story is about two big Afghan tribes, the *Yousefzai* and the *Durrani* who have tribal laws that have a lot in common with Jewish Law. Another name of these tribes is *Pashtunwali.* When I read these amazing stories, I made a vow that one day I would go out on a search for the ten lost tribes.

"I was fascinated by this information and became resolved to go on in an expedition and find the ten lost tribes. Having researched it for a long, I felt that there is still a chance to search for them in distant places. After considering it I decided to start in the range of the Kashmirian Mountains near Afghanistan, the dwelling place of those tribes with Jewish practices. The highest summits in the world are there, and the region is known for being unpopulated and empty. I invested many days in learning the maps of Jammu and Kashmir, the modern main roads, rivers, wildlife, and plants, along with its ancient main roads. I was obsessed with one idea: finding the footsteps of the ten lost tribes.

"After I had completed my research, I approached my father and asked his permission to go on a trip around the world. He asked about where I wanted to go, I simply replied, 'In the footsteps of the ten lost tribes; to State of Jammu and Kashmir in India.'

"My father listened carefully and then asked, 'What are you looking for in these remote places? How can you find the footsteps of tribes that probably ceased to exist thousands of years ago? Why don't you go on a more enjoyable trip to Europe or America? Why risk yourself in a journey to such high and remote areas?'

"For a long time, my father held on with his refusal, but I was resolved and continued to study the maps of the highlands until I knew each and every path there. Finally after asking him for a long time my father consented. I was joyous but still subdued during my preparations in

---

[8] Dagestan in the Caucasus

moving on to fulfill my great dream. The preparations lasted for three months but ended in a very surprising way, as you are about to hear.

"The great day arrived. At the airport, all my family members, including my uncle the bishop, came to see me off. The painful departure ended and I boarded a plane that headed for India — the country that has plenty of religious rites and elephants. My flight was pleasant and I arrived in Delhi, a colorful and joyful city, brimming with large crowds and sacred cows that would walk peacefully in the streets. I had never seen such sights. There I ate a tremendously spicy vegetable sandwich and continued on to the capital of the mountainous state of Jammu and Kashmir. The city of Srinagar is situated in a big valley at the foot of the highest mountain chain in the world. I could hardly believe that my search for the ten lost tribes was about to begin.

"A cold wind that blew fiercely from the mountains penetrated my clothes and froze me. Although It was summer, the eternal snow on the peaks of the mountains reduced the temperatures and it was cool and pleasant. I spent my first day there at a floating hostel on one of the many lakes the city was surrounded with. The floating hostel used to be an old riverboat, like many others that were scattered around the lake, and few of them, for many years, had been laid submerged on its bottom. My dinner I ate with the cook, waiter, steward, and the riverboat skipper — who were actually the same person – the owner of the hostel. He was a short, dark-skinned man, with black, shiny eyes, and who ran diligently and quickly all the tasks of the riverboat as a devil. How had I arrived just at that place I cannot say, but to my great delight this quick-witted man shorty turned to be an infinite source of information about the natives and their customs, their ancestors, and how they arrived in Srinagar which turned out to be very helpful for my journey.

"A week later I departed, and in the early morning took a cab my skipper had ordered for me, a tiny motorcar, patched with many metal sheets. Having arrived at the Central Bus Station I boarded an old rickety bus that stopped just anywhere. Whenever it stopped, the driver announced its destination crying out like a greengrocer in the city market. Many passengers loaded their packages on the bus's roof and stayed there themselves to sit on the roof. In this fashion, we left the Central Bus Station and headed to Ronda, which was a tiny town situated in the middle of the Karakoram Range, or the Black Mountains. The town's houses are built on the banks of a brook that feeds one of the longest rivers on Earth, the Indus River. It flows next to the city's main road that leads to the neighboring country of Afghanistan.

"After all of the passengers were crammed into the old bus, the driver released the handbrake. The bus was speeding downhill … but its engine came back to life coughing and trembling at the last minute like a critically ill person. I found out that sometimes when the bus climbed the mountains, it had to wait for mechanics to bring it back to life. We slowly passed through a valley to the summits of the mountains that were hidden by black clouds. As it ascended, the old dilapidated bus started to make grunting sounds and emitted thick clouds of black smoke that infiltrated into the bus until I became decidedly sick from it.

"The passengers who crammed into the bus swayed in it and occasionally fell onto my seat and pressed me strongly against the wall. From the bus's roof passengers kept looking at me through the windows … laughing and chattering endlessly.

"Each kilometer which was climbed marked a remarkable triumph of the technicians that helped to repair the tin motorized rickety carriage. It unstoppably climbed but at a tortuous pace uphill and stretched its energies to the limit, by pushing and gasping beyond its mechanical capabilities. The road became increasingly poorer with many deep holes and bumps that made both of us - the bus and me - jump up into the air.

"Oh, here comes the end … and we are about to fall to the abyss,' I thought scared to death when I saw how the bus driver tried to hold fast to the steering wheel. I marveled at the calmness of the other passengers who stayed peaceful as nothing was happening.

"The wooden bench on which I was sitting was jumping and screeching under me as if it was about to fall apart any minute. My fear grew higher. Thus, moaning and groaning like an old man near death the bus made its way. There was one moment, when the bus jounced into a deep, wide hole in the middle of the road, that I was high, up in the air, only to land on my rear, and felt as if all my bones were crushed like a vase falling from the top of the mountain.

"But as soon as we started to climb again, my entire troubles were forgotten. The bus passed through sharp curves, along the sides of bottomless abysses. The view of passing along such a narrow road was so dreadful that I began reciting and praying for each and every saint I could remember from school. I also sent many prayers to the God of my forefathers, the Israelites. I kept praying and making vows, but as soon as we arrived safe and sound in the tiny town of Ronda they were entirely forgotten.

"Actually, even with the horrifying experiences with the road, there were quite a few enchanting moments when I celebrated the beautiful towns that were seen from the window, endless waterfalls crashing from above with the snow-covered summits in the background, gigantic trees, an opulent variety of colorful vegetation, the sun that plays hide-and-seek with the clouds and so many other endless of precious gems.

"We arrived at Ronda during the late evening hours. Three streetlights dimly lit the center of the town, built on both sides of a road passing through the center. After a long search, I was pleased to find the largest hostel in the town. It was a poor-looking two-room building made of wood with no restroom or a shower. I swallowed hastily the local food, *chapatti* which is made of rice and I scooped up a lentil soup. And then without delay I went to bed and slept on a mattress filled up with grass, sinking immediately into a deep sleep.

"The following morning I approached the hostel owner, who managed the place barefooted and half-naked. I asked his help in finding a mountain guide for the journey to the heart of the Black Mountains. The next thing I saw from my window was quite odd – dozens of people were gathering sitting just next to my window. In trying to figure out what this gathering was all about, I summoned the owner of the hostel.

" 'Sir has requested to have a guide,' he replied quietly.

" 'That's correct. I want a mountain guide, but not the entire unemployed residents of the town,' I laughed.

"They sat there in sheer silence, waiting for me to come out of my room. Just imagine how difficult it was to select a mountain guide out of so many candidates. I had many questions until I found the right person. It was a tall man named Raja. He explained to me in fluent English that seven porters are needed for the mountain path, so seven people were added to my expedition team.

"When I told Raja that my goal was to look for the footsteps of the ten tribes who were lost here, he stayed calmed and just said seriously, 'It would be a pleasure for me to help you in the quest for your people, but first let's secure the blessing and advice of the Sacred Man.'

" 'The blessing of the Sacred Man!' I exclaimed.

" 'Yes, sir. No one is allowed to climb the holy Karakoram Mountains without the approval of the Sacred Man.'

"The next day I set out and followed Raja, upon the path leading into the mountain range. After four hours of tough hiking with no breaks, we arrived at the home of the Sacred Man. He was dressed in a white robe tall and as thin as a stick. His skin was dry as wood, his big, brown eyes were sunken in their sockets. A few moments later the Sacred Man took an iron pot, piled it with a few herbs, laid it on top of burning cinders, and recited a long series of words that I didn't understand.

"When Raja heard the words of the Sacred Man, he fell to the floor. The Sacred Man continued to whisper his inscrutable words and occasionally threw colorful powders onto the embers, which caused a lot of smoke.

" 'Good journey,' his English was fluent. 'Fear nothing. Nothing to worry about. I have driven all setbacks from your way. In one week from today, you could set out in your journey with the gods' blessings.'

"As soon as he completed his blessing, the Sacred Man took out a green-painted pebble, three seashells, and a small bottle filled with red liquid. 'Keep your charms and they will keep you.'

"Raja stood up, kissed the hands of the Sacred Man, lifted with much care the charms, and whispered to me, 'You should express your respect to the Sacred Man. Give him as many dollars as you wish,' he completed in a half-fainted tone.

"His words about the dollars made me laugh. But I pulled out a ten-dollar bill from my pouch, left it next to his feet, and rushed away.

"When we were on our way back, Raja started, 'There is a legend about a big tribe who arrived at our country many years ago. They climbed into the mountains and disappeared there. The town kids know that it is forbidden to climb on the mountain where the gods dwell. Whenever we wish to climb there, we seek the blessing and advice of the Sacred Man. The fate of anyone who'd attempt to do so without the blessing of the Sacred Man is sealed.'

" 'And now I am going to tell you a story that my grandfather had told me. It happened many years ago when my grandfather was a young herdsman. One day my grandfather tended his herd into the heart of the Black Mountains. My grandfather knew that the Black Mountains were the dwelling place of the gods, but he feared nothing. He thus drove his herd for about two weeks. One day, at sunset, he arrived at a big cave at the foot of the mountain. My grandfather was very happy when he saw the great cave and gathered his entire herd there for the night. Then late at night, he heard terrible noises of crashing rocks. My grandfather woke up alarmed, 'The gods are nibbling the rocks of the mountain. They are probably angry at my trespassing,' He cried.'

" 'And indeed, shortly afterward terrible sounds of thunders were heard and bolts of lightning crossed the sky, lighting up the dark night. A bolt of lightning hit the cave, killing the entire herd that flocked there. My grandfather just stood up shocked and then he only wanted to flee from the wrath of the gods. Ever since then, no one dared to climb to the dwelling of the gods. One day, the Sacred Man appeared in our small town. That was a day of celebration for all the shepherds and thanks to his blessings and charms they could now return to the Sacred Mountains with their herds. This is how I got to know all the roads and footpaths that lead to the Sacred Mountains.'

"While listening to Raja's seemingly ridiculous story, I'd said nothing, but the part about the terrible noise in the cave and the lightning that hit the herd seemed even more bizarre to me. *What could have hit the herd? It's impossible for one bolt to kill an entire herd.*

" 'I would like to visit that cave and then the Bewitched Monastery!'

"Raja looked at me and marveled, 'How do you know about it?'

"Reluctant to say anything else, I only commented that I heard about it from people who had boarded the bus to Ronda.

" 'Sir! There is nothing good about the Bewitched Monastery. People say that anybody entering the monastery will never come out of it. Why is sir looking for trouble? Have some mercy on your young life!'

"After trying to persuade him for a long time, and certainly, after offering him a lot of money, I got Raja to agree to take me to the Bewitched Monastery.

"The following day I started making preparations for my journey to the Black Mountains. Raja and his team worked hard to get the needed food and camping equipment. I took Raja a lot of effort but somehow he managed to get two hunting rifles with some ammunition to protect us against the many beasts in the vast forests that we were about to cross."

Chapter 10

The Journey to the Black Mountains

Mr. D'Acosta continued to speak calmly, "On the seventh day, at sunrise, the journey to the heart of the Black Mountains started. Three yaks loaded with all the equipment required for a long journey stepped behind Raja, who led the expedition cautiously.

"After a short walk on a paved road, we turned north and went down to the river, then headed on a strenuous hike passing through thorny bushes that surrounded us. Sharp thorns stuck on my flesh as poignantly as pins.

"After hiking thus lengthily we arrived at an enormous waterfall and stopped for a short break, which I used for pulling out the many thorns from my flesh. Then we continued until the last rays of sun disappeared and golden-red stretches colored the mountain peaks with their enchanting glory.

"We spent the first night near a smaller waterfall that burst forth rolling its water that emanated from the belly of the earth. I spent my first night listening to the growling sounds of wild beasts, to the calls of nocturnal birds, and to the yelping of the jackals in the forest. Even the three bonfires that we started could not alleviate my fears that the wild beasts were lurking all around us.

"Ready to fire my rifle and alert I passed my first sleepless night in the forest. We were on our feet again before sunrise, got organized fast, and continued with great cautiousness our journey along the river. I was scared to death and my heart pounded strongly when I shot a snake that crossed my way just a few steps from me.

" 'Sir, you shouldn't be scared of snakes. They don't do any harm,' Raja said. Indeed, after a while, I was no longer afraid of the big reptiles. Even a big, threatening crocodile no longer seemed to scare me.

"After another long walk, we entered the thicket of a big forest. Many monkeys were jumping in the trees around us. We heard their screams as we walked through. We were moving slowly, with Raja leading. He used his machete, a long jungle knife, to open up the way. He hit the ferns and plants that blocked our path, causing birds to fly away from the nearby trees.

"Suddenly we heard at a very short distance a growling sound of a bear. Raja stopped and signaled us to stop also. We heard the sound of tree branches breaking nearby and a big gray bear surged in front of us on its rear feet threateningly showing its teeth.

" 'Move back slowly,' Raja said to us quietly. We retreated carefully until we were at a safe distance from the bear.

" 'What are we going to do now?' I was feeling wary.

" 'Nothing to worry about. This is a female bear protecting her cubs. We should bypass this place. We should leave this robust she-bear untouched. Harming one will bring us bad luck.'

"We bypassed the threatening obstacle very carefully and continued on our way. Shortly afterward we left the forest and reached a barren and arid rocky area with no vegetation. We walked with speed through it until dark. At dusk, with the last light, we set up camp. I was very tired and immediately fell asleep. I withdrew into the land of dreams. This time my sleep was not disturbed by the night sounds; all things just faded away ... and I emerged from it reinvigorated and smiled at the rising sun. The more we hiked the stronger I became, until I could easily climb the high mountains. On many occasions, we encountered exotic unfamiliar wildlife that I had seen before only in photographs.

"After twenty-one more days we reached a very tall waterfall, splashing noisily into the lake underneath it. I stood there at length without moving; marveling at the sight of the waterfall that rolled its water to the lake with its jets spraying their mists around. Songbirds filled the air with their wonderful chirping and I inhaled the splendid scents of herbs. For a moment I felt like I was in heaven. We stayed in this wonderful place for two days that I won't ever forget.

"With the first rays of sunlight, we rushed to pack up and started to hike again on the path leading to the summit. Thin rain started to sprinkle over our heads. The path became increasingly poor. Boulders, that had fallen, occasionally blocked our way and forced us to look for alternative paths. The cold wind and immense elevation weighed down on us with each step that we took. Fortunately, yaks cannot complain about the tough terrain. For three days we climbed ascending the steep slopes of the high mountain. We frequently had to pull the yaks with their yokes whenever they refused to continue the arduous trip. Many times, in the crossing of obstacles, Raja had to cover the eyes of the yaks and secure them so that they wouldn't lose their nerves due to these sights.

"It turned out that Raja was an excellent leader and pathfinder and I was pleased about choosing him. In a similar fashion, the other team members were superb and I admired them for their fitness and unusual resilience in carrying the heavy loads. When we arrived at the top of the mountain range, we were once again able to walk comfortably. The bare mountaintop was easy for hiking. After four more days we started down the mountain's northern slope. Gushes of harsh winds thrust at our backs, pushing us down the mountain. Sometimes we were shrouded in heavy fog that made it impossible to see the back of the person that walked in front.

"After a further two days, we arrived at a stream that reeled its water quickly down the slope. After a long break on the banks of the stream, and laying down enjoying the sunlight from the sun that peeked every now and then from behind the fast-moving clouds above, we continued along the stream with renewed vigor.

"Three more days of hastened hiking, have brought us to a cliff that stood as upright as a wall against the mountainside. 'Why did we come to this place? Where are we going now?' I asked Raja impatiently.

" 'Follow the stream!' Raja answered smiling peacefully as he stepped into the stream, which reached the height of his waist. He continued to walk in the stream until he reached the opening where the stream emerged from the mountainside and quickly disappeared inside. A moment later he reappeared from the opening and said, 'It's time to get ready to cross the mountain to its other side!'

"Raja tied the three yaks to nearby trees, took the heavy loads off their backs, and then took out a few torches and handed them to his group members and, now following the porters, he marched toward the tiny opening, and I followed his footsteps.

"Indeed, as time went by, I'd learned to trust Raja and realized how knowledgeable he was in his work. However, I had some doubts when I entered the cold water and followed him. And thus, I found myself walking into a long tunnel, illuminated by the light of the torches that Raja and his team carried. The stream water was cold as ice reaching as high as my chest. Bats that dwelled there, were disturbed and flew excitedly, screaming over our heads. We had a long walk inside the tunnel, which occasionally was just a little bit higher than our heads.

"Walking for so long in the cold water almost paralyzed my body. Finally, the sight of a distant flickering light encouraged me and signaled that we were approaching the exit. And indeed, shortly afterward we exited at the other end of the tunnel directly into a pond. We climbed out of the pond and found ourselves on a ledge. Just three steps ahead of me I saw a terrible abyss and a monastery carved into the mountainside across from me and behind the abyss.

" 'The Bewitched Monastery!' Raja whispered with awe. 'Down there, not too far from the monastery, is the big cave where my grandfather heard the voices of the angry gods that hit his flock with a lightning bolt. But we took another way to reach the cave. This is another way that leads to the monastery.'

" 'How are we going to cross such an abyss?' I asked in amazement.

" 'There is a bridge not too far from here, leading to the monastery.'

" 'A bridge?! Who built a bridge in such a place?' I exclaimed with amazement.

" 'This is a very old bridge. It is made of very strong forest bushes. You will soon see it, soon with your own eyes.'

"After drying out and warming up by the heat of a small fire, we continued carefully to descend along a narrow winding path with the abyss alongside us. From a distance I saw a bridge made of ropes, swinging like a drunken person in the strong wind. 'Hey! Unbelievable!' I remarked all excited, 'How could anyone cross on such a circus swing?'

"The bridge swung so strongly that it seemed about to fly off and drop down into the abyss. 'Raja, my good friend, please tell me the truth. How can we possibly cross this dreadful bridge safely?' I asked in a trembling voice."

" 'My intelligent friend, my father and my grandfather both crossed this bridge.'

" 'What?' I said, extremely scared. 'Can't you see that the moment you'd place your two feet on this circus bridge, you will have a family reunion with your forefathers?'

" 'My esteemed sir, look,' Raja smiled briefly and immediately climbed onto the bridge, gleefully jumping on it, and then headed on across it very quickly.

"I closed my eyes quickly, waiting for bad news. But then I heard Raja's voice from the other side of the mountain, calling me. I opened my eyes and saw him standing on the far end of the bridge jumping on it as if there were no gaping abyss below him. However, even his act of bravery did not convince me to cross this swaying circus ladder of a bridge.

"After I made several attempts, that ended unsuccessfully, to step onto the bridge, Raja ran back over the bridge. Upon arrival, he took a handkerchief out of his pocket, tied it around my head, and with my eyes covered he announced, 'Now, sir is going to follow me.'

"With shaking legs and a fast-beating heart I followed him. I can find no words to describe the intense fear I felt until I stepped off the swaying rope bridge and stood on the firm stony ground on the other side of the abyss.

"Yells of excitements were heard from the team at the other side who then rushed across the bridge following me.

" 'Now, esteemed sir, it is our time to depart,' said Raja. 'We are not going to continue to the Bewitched Monastery. We will return now to the camp where we left the yaks. We will be waiting there for you for one month. If sir does not return one month from now, we will return to our homes sad. From this place onwards you are going to climb alone to the monastery.'

"My pleading to them to come with me up at least to the gates of the monastery didn't help. The only option left for me was to depart from Raja and his team. I paid them their sum and started to walk up to the path leading to the monastery. With small steps, I climbed up the mountain while Raja's image became smaller and smaller until I could no longer see him. I have never seen him again since that day.

"*Are there any people in the monastery? Who are they? What is their faith? Will they help me to find descendants of the ten lost tribes? Will I be able to return without Raja's help?* With each step I took, my thoughts accumulated as if they were amassing into a mountain of unanswerable questions.

Chapter 11

The Bewitched Monastery

"It's hard to find words that express what I felt as I headed toward the monastery. My sense of fear increased and my heart was beating wildly. Regret filled my mind and I started to doubt whether I had made a mistake when I decided to go on a search for tribes that had disappeared thousands of years ago. However, notwithstanding all my fears, I did not stop climbing up the mountain. The scenery was breathtaking. Below me, over the abyss, I saw the rope bridge, swaying in the blowing winds.

"I continued up the mountain. The strenuous journey has strengthened the muscles in my body and legs. I no longer felt the exhaustion I had during the first few days of the journey. Finally, I approached a stone building near the monastery and examined it carefully. It appeared abandoned. It was intended for ghosts only I thought.

"I climbed onto the roof of the abandoned building from where I can get a good observation point to view the monastery that was hewn into the mountainside not far from where I stood.

"On the mountainside, a vertical stone wall, I noticed dozens of tiny decorated openings that were surrounded by a beautiful relief. I quickly climbed down from the roof of the abandoned building and rushed toward the Bewitched Monastery. I stood fascinated in front of the monastery. A very narrow path led up to the opening, which was about sixty meters above me.

"*Who built this wonderful thing? Is there life in it?* I pondered and climbed carefully up the path.

"Cold winds started to blow, and mist began to blanket the area. 'Anybody? Is there anybody there?' I called out loud. Echoes of my voice returned from the mountains. No reply was heard except the howling sounds of the wind as if it was mocking my question. The now heavy mist covered the opening until I could hardly see the narrow path any longer.

"After a long, slow climb I reached what seemed to be an opening. How disappointed I was when I discovered that actually, it was only a nice decoration in the shape of a door. For a long time, I observed the handful of tiny openings above my head and asked myself how they could be reached.

"*I am not going to go back until I find a way to enter this monastery*, I made a vow to myself. I walked back and forth alongside the mountainside, looking for a way up to the openings, but my searches were of no avail. I looked in vain for an explanation for the feigned door.

"Darkness fell and I set up my shelter-half and got into my sleeping bag. With the light of dawn, I took out the mountain climbing gear. I tried to climb up to the tiny openings, but all my attempts to thrust wedges into the rocky mountainside failed as well as some stratagems I had been taught by Raja. I considered climbing to the top of the mountain and then climb down into the tiny openings, but this was too dangerous, so I decided against it.

"With remorseful feelings, I spent my second night at the foot of the Bewitched Monastery. I turned from side to side but was unable to fall asleep. Suddenly the night sky became clear of clouds and the moon spilled its light onto the monastery. I got up and looked at the moon floating peacefully in the sky. A sound of moving stones nearby alarmed me, and I tried to figure out what made this noise, but couldn't see anything. Suddenly a large gorilla came from somewhere behind me and stood right in front of me. My legs were trembling. I was sure that this dreadful gorilla was about to tear me to pieces as a cat would do to a mouse. For a moment I saw a human look in the gorilla's eyes and for a moment its face looked very much like a human's face, with a unique mocking look in its eyes. After a few seconds that seemed to me like an eternity, then suddenly it disappeared in one jump while emitting a sharp scream. After recovering from this bloodcurdling encounter, I went back to my tent and somehow immediately fell asleep.

"Heavy rain and stormy weather welcomed me on the morning of the third day. When it stopped for a moment, I left my tent, sat on a big rock, and pondered my situation. My head in my hands with despair. The rain resumed and poured down intensely, but I felt nothing. *What am I going to do? Maybe my father was right when he objected to my plans. Perhaps I did things not in the right way — is it possible to find tribes that were lost thousands of years ago? There is no way to climb up to this monastery. I must return right now! Perhaps looking in other areas can help? In other monasteries?*

"I felt a hand on my shoulder and sprang to my feet. I turned around quickly and saw an old man in a white robe, with a turban on his head, a long white beard, and an eminent mustache on his face.

"His smiling face reassured me. He gestured for me to follow him. I quickly gathered my stuff and followed as if hypnotized. The man reached the mountain wall and disappeared into it. I stopped unable to believe my eyes. Perhaps I was losing my mind and following a ghost? After all, human beings cannot possibly go through walls.

"Then the man suddenly came out of the mountainside, took my hand, and pulled me after him. Before I could shout that I didn't want to go through the wall, don't want all this madness, I passed through the wall and found myself behind it, without hearing the slightest sound. The strange transformation left me bewildered with my mouth gaped. *What just happened? Did I pass through the wall or not? And what happened during my passing?* For a long time, I stood amazed in front of a long tunnel, lit with a bluish daylight. *This must be the secret opening to the Bewitched Monastery!* I started walking hesitantly. After a short walk, we entered a large room; the door closed behind us. I was surprised when I felt the room quickly moving upward. Was it an elevator? Who could possibly believe that one would find a sophisticated elevator in this remote place?

"A moment later the elevator stopped. I could see, through the open door, a long narrow hallway painted in bright green and lit up with the same bluish daylight. The old man walked slowly while I followed him. After several minutes of walking along multiple long corridors, we reached a door painted in the same shade of green as the corridor.

"The old man opened the door, signaled me to remain in place, and disappeared behind the door. A few minutes later he reappeared and gestured me to enter. In a large room, around a large wooden table, three persons were sitting, with their bearings similar to that of the old man who had attended to me.

"One of the men turned to me and said, 'Hello, Mr. Arthur D'Acosta.' *How do they know my name? How is it possible?* 'We have been waiting for you for a long time. Welcome!' he continued to speak in fluent Spanish. 'Will you please tell these Masters here who you are and why you are looking for the ten lost tribes?'

"After concluding his speech he stood up, placed a white cape over my shoulders, and a blue turban on my head. 'As of this moment, you are one of our own family, and only death can part us,' he said. His words made my emotions run high.

"I stood in front of them for a long time, telling my story. However, I followed my father's advice and did not reveal our family secret about being part of a family of Marranos. 'As a researcher of ancient peoples, I decided to find out what had happened to the ten lost tribes. This is the reason why I arrived at this desolated place,' I concluded.

"'And why are you looking for them so far away?' the man asked.

"'After a long period of research, I reached the conclusion that the ten lost tribes, who had been exiled from their homeland, made their way to remote and hidden places where they could avoid being hurt by the cruelty of the human beast. It is obvious that the ten lost tribes did not just vanish into thin air. They probably live in a hidden place and have kept themselves safe.'

"The three Masters listened to me very carefully, with strange smiles on their faces. After telling my story, I repeated my question as to how did they know about my name and the objective of my visit.

"After hearing my question they just smiled again from ear to ear but didn't say a word. They just stood up, bowed to me, and left through a nearby door. My old companion signaled me to follow him as he entered a nearby room. Shoes, blankets, clothes, and all the supplies a man needs were arranged on wooden shelves. A few moments later, I left the room holding two white robes, two blue turbans, and a pair of wooden sandals. I followed the man again, to a staircase that led to the upper floor. We went upstairs, passed through a hall with approximately twenty side-rooms, and entered the last room.

"My companion gestured that this was my room. For a long time, I looked around my new place. The room was hewn into the mountain rock, as were the adjacent rooms. A large wooden bed with a straw mattress sat in the corner. A square table with two shabby-looking chairs was in the center. In a box near the table, I found a knife, fork, spoon, large metal cup, and white china plate.

"Before I could become accustomed to this new place, my companion was back accompanied by another man who was holding a sharp knife and a large tin bowl. Quickly, my long hair dropped into the bowl. As soon as these two people left my room, I looked in the mirror and saw my bald head. My spirit sank to the sight of my bald head. It was dreadful as well as amusing. I would have never believed that one day I would look like an onion. It didn't take long till I found my onion head most amusing and I even burst out in laughter; slightly easing my gloomy state of mind.

"*Here's to you. You looked for the ten lost tribes and you've got a monastery full of silent monks, a blue turban, a glorious onion head,* I said to myself, laughing.

"After I relaxed a little from the blandness of my new appearance, I started to feel sad again. *What will happen now? Will I end my life in this remote monastery of the Silent Monks? What will my parents, my brother, and the rest of my family think? They will never find me. Why did the monks say that I was a member of their family? What sect do they belong to?* With so many questions going through my mind, I became very tired. I got into my new bed and immediately fell asleep.

"The sound of a bell ringing woke me from my sound sleep. I opened my eyes and saw my old companion standing in the room waiting patiently while I'd got dressed and got ready. This was my new daily routine that continued for many more days: first waking up at sunrise, then washing in cold water and eating breakfast, and finally going out to work. I did a variety of chores, such as laundry, painting, various repairs in the building, and some other jobs I had never done before.

"After a few days, I learned that twenty-one people were living there. However, I didn't see the three old men who welcomed me around. I kept wondering where they had disappeared to but could not get an answer for that.

"The library turned out to be a nice surprise for me. In a large room, filled with many isles of shelves, containing books in many languages. I became quite soon familiar with the three levels of the monastery library. But some things remained unexplained. How did the monks receive a supply of fresh food? What was the source of the strange light that lit up the halls and rooms? The list of questions just grew from day to day and tortured me during many sleepless nights. I repeatedly asked myself what really was happening here and if the monastery was really bewitched?

"At the end of the third week, I decided to start searching for answers to the many bothering questions on my mind. One day, after I finished lunch, I went back to my room and did not go down to the library as I usually did. Thirty minutes later, when I realized that no one was following me, I decided to look for secret rooms and for the storeroom of the fresh food. However, after many hours of extensive searching, I had not found anything. I made my way back to my room, in a morbid state of mind.

Chapter 12

The Maze of Tunnels

"Another month went by. All my questions remained unanswered. I couldn't find a clue of what was going on inside the monastery. But at the beginning of the third month, I encountered something that increased my excitement and curiosity. It was shortly after lunch, that I went down to the library as usual, to my great surprise I found a Hebrew newspaper that, according to the date on it, had been printed in Jerusalem that very day! *How did the newspaper get to this remote place so fast?* I wondered. I felt that I must leave no stone unturned until I found the answers to my questions.

"At the crack of dawn I started preparing for my great search, and after a short breakfast, I began. For hours I carefully checked every corner of the maze of hallways and rooms, but all my efforts were for nothing. Then the memory of the elevator came to mind and I paced quickly through the hallways until I found it. Entering the elevator I looked in vain for the control panel, but I couldn't find it. I stood there and tried to remember the way I took it up for the first time with my elder companion, but I recalled nothing.

"Another act of witchcraft! 'Please let me out of this damn monastery!' I said loudly. Before I could finish my words, the door closed and the elevator went down very quickly.

"I stood engulfed in amazement by this new magic. When the elevator door opened wide again, I rushed out and quickly turned toward the exit hallway. *Escape … I want to escape from this crazy place*, I thought, walking faster. But the exit was blocked and neither my angry shouts nor my banging on it helped me to get out of there. I was about to go back when I saw two small openings of burrows, a few steps away from me. If animals used these burrows as a hiding place, then they must lead outside of the monastery. I looked closely at the burrows: The first was narrow and long; the other one was slightly larger and wider. I felt that I must get inside the second burrow. I threaded my body into the bigger one, turned on my compact flashlight, and started to crawl.

"After crawling for a while I reached a place where the burrow split into three directions. In the dim light, all the burrows looked similar. A mossy smell was hanging in the air, and a sense of fear started to creep into my heart. Hesitatingly I decided to take the one to the right. I crawled slowly until I reached a wide space where I was almost able to stand upright. I looked around but could not find anything of interest. Finally, I made my way back.

"When I entered the elevator, I exclaimed, 'Up, please.' The door closed immediately, and the elevator went up quickly. I was exhausted but very happy when I went back to my room. After I took a shower and changed my clothes, I went down to the library. It seemed as if no one acknowledged me when I sat next to the large table; it was as if my absence had passed completely unnoticed.

"The following day I changed my robe, put on my clothes and shoes, and went back to the burrows. After I crawled quickly, I reached the location where I had stopped the previous day and from there I needed to bend in order to proceed. I suddenly noticed that the ceiling of the tunnel was hewn. You probably understand the meaning of it: a hewn stone is something made by man, not by a digging mammal. I continued to crawl until I arrived at a point where the tunnel turned again into a narrow and low burrow, and then I started to crawl on my belly.

"Crawling was very difficult. I could hardly find my way. My efforts to turn back were unsuccessful. After a brief attempt to crawl backward, I realized that I was stuck so I continued forward deeper into the burrow. The thought that I might not be able to turn around scared me greatly. I crawled slowly on my stomach and couldn't see the end of the tunnel. Several times the sense of despair overcame me, but I was able to quickly recover from it and continue my slow, annoying crawl.

"After a few hours that seemed like an eternity, I reached the end of this narrow burrow. Finally, I was able to stand upright and accelerate my pace. I no longer wanted to return. I hastened my steps and started walking quickly toward the unknown.

"Now I noticed that the burrow became spacious and more like a tunnel; I could hardly reach the ceiling when I raised my hand. Tiny streams of water were dripping from the ceiling, making it difficult to walk, but I did not stop and continued with renewed energies.

"Suddenly I saw a thin beam of light flickering in front of me. For a moment I thought it was an optical illusion, but when I turned my flashlight off I could see the beam of light clearly twinkling like a star high in the sky. How happy I was to see this thin beam of light. With my heart pounding strongly I approached the light as it kept strengthening.

"I arrived at a wide opening of a large luxurious hall that was lit with bluish daylight. A large stone table and two stone benches were at the center of the hall. Above all, I was intrigued to notice a dozen large openings carved into the cave walls.

"I stood amazed at this new discovery. *Who were the people that used to live here? Who dug the long burrows that led away from the hall and where do they lead to?* The heavy layer of dust that covered the hall indicated clearly that the place had been abandoned for many years. *Why would they have left, and where did they go?*

"After examining the hall and looking into the burrows that were centripetally forked from it, I decided to turn back. My flashlight was beginning to weaken and I was concerned about finding my way back.

"Back at the Bewitched Monastery I spent the next three days searching for an alternative source of light but I couldn't find one.

However, I was no longer afraid to disappear for many hours. No one asked any questions or seemed to notice my long absences. I felt free as a bird.

"The mere idea of not having a source of light inside the burrows depressed me. I made some efforts to preserve oil from my meals and I prepared an improvised oil lamp from a tin can and a piece of cloth that I dipped in the oil.

"The following day I went down the elevator and entered one of the burrows. It didn't take much for the black smoke coming out of the makeshift oil lamp to penetrate my nostrils. My head rolled in despair when I made my way back to my room. But it did not discourage me. A hectic passion to search for a flashlight was burning in my soul. I focused my entire thoughts on the issue of finding a flashlight to continue my search.

"After considerable thought, I mustered enough courage and wrote down a request to my original 'companion', the epithet I gave to the monk who took care of me in the monastery. My companion read what I wrote very intently; then he turned around and went away. The frozen look on his face made me understand that my request would be denied. I was then surprised that he approached me very soon and placed a paper-wrapped object on my hand. As he left I noticed a smile flashing for a brief second on his frozen face.

"I looked at the object, which was wrapped in paper. I removed the paper and saw a black square box with a red glass eye in its center. I examined the box from all its sides but there was no 'on' push button on it. Suddenly I noticed a small note glued onto the wrapping paper, and I read it: 'If you want to turn the flashlight to 'on' or 'off', ask that in your heart.'

"I have never heard of anyone who'd had a decent conversation with a flashlight. I had a hearty laugh about it. I said in my heart, *Trial number one: Let there be light!* As soon as I uttered my request a glimmering bluish light appeared and lightened up the room as if in daylight. It took some time until I recovered from my new discovery. Then I rushed back to the elevator, anxious to pass through the burrows again and return to the big hall.

"Over the next few days, I prepared some accurate maps of the network of tunnels and burrows that branched underneath the mountain. For some months I continued to crawl and wander around in them and copied new ones to my maps. One morning I woke up and I lost the motivation to continue my searches through the long burrows and tunnels that seemed to lead to nowhere. *What else is left for me to do in this place?* I was plagued by despair.

"*This is it,* I said to myself. *I have reached the end of my way in the Bewitched Monastery. It has stopped to be bewitching anyway ... as a matter of fact, it's no more than an endless network of burrows and tunnels. And here in this desolated place all of my dreams are about to end, and no one will ever know where I have disappeared to.* 'Noooooo!' my terrible cry cut the silence around me, 'I would be better if I'd find my death on the mountains around here, fall into an abyss or become a prey to the wild beasts, rather than end my life in this remote place.'

"I jumped out of my bed and went out looking for my companion. 'Sir, please, I want to leave the monastery right away!' I exclaimed when I found him. My excitement was peaking in me. 'I can't stay here for even one more minute!'

Chapter 13

On the Main Road

"My companion was not at all impressed with my screaming. He took out a pen and paper, wrote down a few words, gave me the paper, and went away. I opened the folded piece of paper and read: 'Get ready for a meeting with the three masters tomorrow early at dawn.'

"And indeed, as soon as I woke up, my companion appeared and gestured me to follow him. I followed him quickly. We soon arrived in a large room. Through the open door, I could see the three Masters sitting around a table.

" 'What is your wish, our young brother, Arthur D'Acosta?' one of the Masters asked in Spanish.

" 'Esteemed Masters. The only thing I ask is to leave the monastery and continue my search for the ten lost tribes. I don't want to be a monk. Please, help me get out of here!' I said in one breath.

"The Master who was sitting at the center cracked a big smile. 'Our young brother, no one is going to stop you. You are free to leave the monastery right away if you wish. However, you should know that the road is extremely hard, and without a guide, you might get lost in the high mountains or disappear into one of the abysses on these highland ranges that stretch beyond the horizon. Young man! Where are you rushing to go to? Think about what you are going to do and don't rush! Many surprises might await you along the way! We will meet again in a few months. Remember: by trying patiently and thoughtfully you'll achieve your goal.' As the Master finished his words, a mysterious smile hovered over his face.

"The last sentence and the mysterious smile had both subdued my anger and my desire to escape. Something of the words, 'by trying patiently and thoughtfully you'll achieve your goal,' let me think that there is more here than met the eye and that 'being patient pays'. *Do these people have something in common with the ten lost tribes?* A gut feeling informed me that, *yes, they have.*

"Twenty-four hours had passed since my meeting, and I reinitiated my search with renewed energies. I felt that this time my chances to find a clue were significant. The words, 'by trying patiently and thoughtfully you'll achieve your goal,' kept buzzing in my head as I returned to the long burrows, and searched for an answer to the mystery of the place.

"One day I arrived at the great hall, where I had already been many times before, and walked toward the big stone table and stone benches around it. Suddenly the question struck me, *how were such a large stone table and benches installed in this place? The opening here is not wide enough for such a large table to get through,* I was amazed. *That they are here means there must be a hidden large opening somewhere and a wide tunnel around. How could I miss it? There must be a secret opening somewhere in the wall of this hall!*

"I celebrated my newly-gained insight and jumped with joy. Then I picked a big stone off the floor and started to hit the walls vigorously all around the hall. *If there is an empty space behind them I will hear a dim sound,* I thought while I was hitting the walls. I completed encircling the hall whilst intensely hitting the walls, but couldn't hear anything different.

" 'The hell with it!' I yelled angrily and flung my stone at the opposite wall. Miraculously, and unexpectedly, a prolonged dim sound reverberated around the room, and deafened my eardrums. I froze with amazement at the sound of the metallic echo. 'This is the hidden wall,' I called out loud, rushing toward the spot where the stone had hit.

"To my great surprise, I discovered that it hit exactly at a height that I could reach with my hand. I quickly lifted the stone and hit the same spot again. The metallic sound was heard again, very clearly. *Bingo! Spot on!*

"After many attempts I smashed the thick plaster layer, revealing a copper plate behind it. All my efforts to continue to uncover the copper plate failed. I made my way back to the monastery to look for a small ladder and a few tools. I had to apply for help again from my companion and wrote him my request. Without saying a word and in a placid manner, he took my hand and led me to the monastery's tool storage room where I found everything I needed. Then I made my way back to the hall.

"Crawling with the equipment was strenuous. I reached the hall extremely tired with sweat all over my body. After a short break and drinking some water, I placed the ladder against the wall and, with the help of a small hammer and chisel, started to remove the plaster from the copper plate. It was hard work but finally, I uncovered a large wooden door covered with copper plates. I was pleased to see that the door opened without any effort.

"Upon opening the door I saw a very clean tunnel, lighted in the bluish colors of daylight. Without hesitation, I climbed up and entered the tunnel. I just took a few steps and arrived at a pair of sizeable niches inside which I saw dozens of smaller niches hewn into the rock. Hesitantly I entered one of the main ones, walking quickly past the smaller niches carved within the big one. Now I understood that it was a catacomb and that its smaller niches were filled with elegant-looking sarcophagi[9].

"I left the catacomb and continued to walk along the tunnel. Thirty steps later I reached a small curve that was blocked by a stone wall. I knew that I had to go back and look around the sarcophagi to find out who was buried in such sumptuous-looking coffins. Certainly, they were either high-ranking or very wealthy people. One way or another, I had to find some information about these people.

---

[9] Sarcophagus was an ancient burial coffins made of stone; Catacombs were burial caves in ancient times

"After some consideration, I decided to open a few of the coffins. I stuck the iron chisel under a heavy stone cover that had been placed on the coffin and forcefully pushed it away with both of my legs. The stone covering shifted slightly and a tiny opening appeared, making it possible to peek inside. I rushed to pick up the flashlight and directed its light through the tiny opening. I saw a human skeleton on the bottom of the coffin. A bag made of leather lay next to it.

"I picked it up and after some more effort, I managed to make a few cuts in the leather bag and pulled out a scroll made of papyrus[10] that was in a good condition. I was swept by a sensation of awe and started to jump anxiously and joyously around the coffin for a couple of minutes. The next thing I did was to sing the words of the Barber from Seville that I sang from the bottom of my heart. After I calmed down, I pushed my hand through and pulled out more of the scrolls that I could see through the narrow slit in the bag. I picked them carefully and opened one of them with much care. I gently wiped the fine dust off its surface, and in front of my hypnotized eyes emerged the familiar letters of the ancient Hebrew script.

"The discovery sent a shiver down my spine and I mumbled to myself, 'Ancient Hebrew writing! How did these scrolls get here? Is he a member of the Jewish nation? Have I found a place where the ten lost tribes passed on their way? 'By trying patiently and thoughtfully you'd achieve your goal'. Was the old Master referring to this revelation? Does he know what is buried in the ancient graves?'

"I don't remember how I made my way back to the Bewitched Monastery, with the bag containing the scrolls. For many days I felt like I was intoxicated from my sensational discovery and spent many hours staring at the bag containing the treasure. I took the first scroll and with shaking hands opened it. With great effort, I could spread out the scroll and started to translate it. Fortunately, I was quite savvy in ancient Hebrew script, and my knowledge turned to be very helpful.

"The translation of the scrolls took much time even though the writing was very clear. The first scroll started was a commercial contract between two people. It included oaths in the name of God not

---

[10] Papyrus = ancient parchment

to breach the contract. I was so captivated by the translation process that for three days and three nights I worked on it without eating and almost fainted from hunger and thirst. The varied assortment of scrolls included commercial contracts, marriage licenses – Ketubah – and some written oaths and vows. The more my self-confidence grew, the faster I translated. Early at dawn of the third morning, following a marathon of working on the translations, I realized how tired I was. My eyes closed and I slipped into a world of dreams. After many hours of troubled sleep, I woke up and went straight into the dining room but no one seemed to notice me or ask where I had been.

"After completing a big meal I immediately resumed my translation work. It was almost midnight that in one scroll that I had translated I found a variety of drawings of designs and the names of the ten lost tribes! This discovery made me so excited that I stood up and started to jump with elation like a frantic, bitten billy-goat, 'I am getting into the main road!'

Chapter 14

Additional Discoveries

“I held Hebrew parchment scrolls that listed names of the ten lost tribes. These were the first signs that I was on the right track following the footsteps of the ten lost tribes. I was overwhelmed with a wave of wonderings: *Are there any more scrolls in the tombs? How did the ten lost tribes come here and where did they go to? Did they settle down nearby or continued in their wanderings far from here? Where does the blocked tunnel lead to? How can I find a passage behind the wall to more tunnels and catacombs?* At dusk, I completed my translation work, but I didn't get any significant new information from it.

“After I filled my rumbling hungry stomach, I walked slowly toward my tiny room. I was almost there, absorbed in deep thoughts about the amazing findings when I felt a hand touching my shoulder. I turned my head and there I saw my ‘old companion’ gesturing to me to follow him.

“Had my secret been noticed? Would the scrolls be taken away from me? Would my research work be banned, and I'd be expelled and die in the mountains? With all these questions racing in my mind, I entered the room where the three Masters had welcomed me on my first day. However, the room was empty. As soon as we entered, the floor started to sink rapidly. Suddenly it stopped and a large corridor lit by bluish daylight emerged in front of my eyes. 'What is this place?' I asked my companion. His frozen face and tight lips revealed nothing.

"I followed him with my mind busily wondering and doubting him. We passed along the corridor and went into a large hall with many isles with long shelves that were loaded with books. It was the largest library I have ever seen. My companion passed through this hall to the other side, to another corridor with many rooms on both sides. At the twelfth room on the right, my companion stopped, opened the door, and, with a slight gesture, invited me to enter.

"It was a very well-furnished room with expensive wall-to-wall carpeting covering the floor. An antique table and a set of expensive-looking armchairs were in the center, and many other valuable artifacts were on display. Suddenly a curtain on the opposite wall moved and an old man wearing a white beard and a robe stepped directly toward me. The man shook my hand warmly, asking in good Spanish how I was. As in the tradition of my father's family, my answer was brief and polite. In return for my politeness, the old man responded with a smile and asked me to sit opposite him.

"The man glanced at me and asked, 'Tell me, esteemed mister, why you chose to come to this remote place?' Again I repeated my life story at length, but once again, according to my father's advice, I refrained from hinting that I was a member of the Marranos.

" 'Why are you interested in the fate of Jewish tribes that disappeared two thousand and seven hundred years ago? Why do you believe that it is possible to find the ten lost tribes after so many years? If they do exist somewhere, why didn't they return to their homeland?' He asked me after I was done.

" 'When I studied Middle Eastern Studies at university,' I replied. 'I became acquainted with the fascinating story of the ten lost tribes, who were exiled by the Assyrian invaders and have never been seen again. Only the tribes of Judah and Benjamin were left out of the original twelve. I delved into excessive research on the Jewish nation and it dawned at me that these peoples are guarded by a mysterious power from annihilation. Other peoples from antiquity in the area have disappeared, leaving behind the ruins of their homes and sumptuous palaces. The Jewish nation was the only one to survive to this day despite persecutions that plagued amongst others, my homeland, Spain.

My country played a central role in persecuting them. However, this terrible suffering did not break the spirit of the Jewish nation. After 2,000 years in the Diaspora, it has returned to its homeland and made the desert blossom. This is why I believe that the ten lost tribes were not wiped off the face of the world. They are definitely hiding in some remote places where they will not be hurt by the cruelty of either humans or beasts.'

"When the old man heard my answer he smiled from ear to ear and started, 'Excellent answer, my educated man.' He stood on his feet with excitement. 'And now I am going to give you additional and valuable material. This material includes information that is even more revealing than the scrolls you have found so far. Your actions have not been concealed and I know about everything that happens in this place. I'm congratulating you for your kind deeds. From this day onwards, you are permitted to enter here whenever it fits you. The big library is at your disposal. By trying patiently and thoughtfully you'll achieve your goal.' He shook my hand warmly and stepped behind the curtain.

"I stood up. When I turned around, I found that my companion had disappeared too. I was intrigued and moved the curtain aside — but I saw behind it only a stone wall.

"I sat on one of the chairs resting my head on my two hands. This was, indeed, a very strange place, where people were disappearing behind walls, strange daylight lightning rooms permanently with no source of electricity, and fresh food being served every day although it is such a desolated place. *What is the secret of this place?* 'I'm going to give you additional and valuable material', the old man's words echoed in my ears. I knew that I still had a long way to go until I could crack the secret of the Bewitched Monastery, its ancient sarcophagi, and mysterious documents.

"Many days had passed since my encounter with the old man. I went daily to the big library and immersed myself in the incredible variety of books I found there. As time went by, I forgot all about the catacombs, the tunnels, the burrows, and even the scrolls.

"One day, as I sat in the big library facing a tall pile of books, I heard the sound of approaching steps. I raised my head and saw an unfamiliar young man. He stopped by my table and handed me a note that read: 'Please follow the holder of this letter.' I followed him to the large room where to my great surprise he closed the curtain then opened it and behind it, I saw a wide opening. Just a minute ago there was only a wall at that same place. I didn't hesitate and followed him through the opening into a grand hallway. After taking a few steps, we went down the stairs to the opening of a poor-looking tunnel and continued quickly through it until we arrived at a crossing point of four narrow and lower tunnels that branched out from there. Being slightly above my head we continued to walk carefully to the one that was across from us.

"After passing it we arrived at a wide cave. When I raised my head I was able to see dozens of small niches hewn into the cave walls. I was extremely excited at the sight of the menorah, a symbol of the Jewish nation embedded in the mosaic floor of the cave. Now I had no doubt that I was standing at a place where members of my people had once lived.

"My companion prepared to depart from me by lowering his head and turned to leave. 'Sir, please stop and tell me who are you? What is this strange place? Please tell me!' The young man paused, looked at me with his piercing eyes, and went away with a wide smile on his face.

"I stayed put there, examining the cave at length. I instinctively placed my hand in the nearby niche. The papyrus that I pulled out suggested that this was an ancient archive with an enormous treasure of scrolls. I spent many days returning to this secret place and reading the enormous number of scrolls.

"Absorbed with the translation of the many scrolls, I forgot about the world outside. One day I discovered a papyrus with some incomprehensible words. It took many days to decipher it; only then I could grasp the great significance of this scroll. And I hereby present you with its translation:

> Not many days have passed since we arrived at the Great Cave, and there were bolts of lightning, fire, pillars of smoke, and much loud thunder. We cried to our God and told Him that our expulsion from our homeland to this remote land was difficult enough to endure and asked for His forgiveness and mercy.
>
> At the end of twelve months, David Ben David who went on an errand to explore the Land of the Elephant, or India, has returned

to the Great Cave. So he then unfolded all things that happened to him there — the bolts of lightning and pillars of smoke; the carriage of the Good Spirit that can travel through clouds. For that reason inhabitants of the Land of the Elephants began to sacrifice seventy virgins on a fire altar to please the Good Spirit that lives in the Black Mountains. On the 40th day at noon, the God, which is known as the Good Spirit, went up to the sky in a storm of lightning and thunder. And the magicians of the Land of the Elephants gathered and ordered the people to build the Good Spirit a palace so that God will live in it forever.

At the end of three months, the priests of the Good Spirit had brought the holy books that God has given them and presented the Book of Law in front of the people of the Land of the Elephants. After these events, the priests caught tens of thousands of heathens and placed them on an altar to be consumed by fire.

"I read the scroll many times trying to understand, but to no avail. I wondered: *Who were these people that were expelled from the land of their forefathers? What did they see in the sky? What was the carriage that David Ben David had seen in the Land of the Elephants? Where is the Great Cave he returned to and where the Sons of Israel were staying? Is this scroll telling a legend? Or is it the truth? Who was the being they named the Good Spirit?*

"I'd translated the scrolls for many months and after that, I resumed my wanderings through the narrow burrows and tunnels. One day I went down the way leading to the cave with the niches and turned toward a tunnel on the right, which I had never visited before. While I was in the tunnel a strong smell of apples had suddenly caught my nose. It made me walk faster, and shortly afterward I arrived at three large rooms. Hesitantly and carefully I walked toward the first one on the right, and bizarrely I found there a large amount of fresh fruit and vegetables. In the second and third rooms, there was still more food. *I have found where the supply of food is stored in!* I was happy about that. *But where is it coming from?*

"I went back and reached the crossroads point and where I turned toward the tunnel on the left, holding a bunch of bananas in one hand and a red and fragrant apple in my other hand. When I noticed some burial niches on both sides of the tunnel.

"Above the opening of the first niche on the right, I saw an inscription of small letters and the words that were etched in the stone: 'Zvi Ben Yosef, the scribe'. A simple-looking stone sarcophagus was at the center of the niche. *Who is this Zvi Ben Yosef the scribe?* I wondered. With considerable effort, I managed to open slightly the large stone lid. A human skeleton was lying in the sarcophagus with an object that was wrapped in leather next to it.

"Without thinking twice, I pushed my hand in, picked up the wrapped object, and unfolded it with the utmost care. I took my new finding and went my way back.

"And now my friends, you know exactly where I found the notorious diary which you had purchased from the boy."

"Mr. D'Acosta, how did you and your diary made all the way from the Bewitched Monastery to the streets of Old Jerusalem?" I asked.

"Patience, my friends. After completing the translation of the diary, I still had many unsolved questions. *When the diary was written? What is the connection between the Son of the Planets who was revealed to Zvi Ben Yosef the scribe and what was the Good Spirit that the spy, David Ben-David, saw at the Land of the Elephants? Is this diary considered to be a legend too? Is it possible that the Son of the Planets really visited Earth? And if so, then where is he today?*

"Several days later I found a tiny piece of papyrus at the Cave of the Niches that changed my way of thinking and convinced me that the documentation of the scribe's words in the diary is true. The translation of this document is as follows:

To my brothers, the Sons of Israel: I therein pronounce to your ears that I, the son of the scribe Zvi Ben Yosef, clarify henceforth that everything that my father had said before he passed away is lies and sheer nonsense. My father has never met the Son of the Planets. He had never received anything from him and obviously, knew nothing about the hidden location of the Tables of the Law in the Temple of Jerusalem.

"I was now convinced that the skeleton inside the catacomb was that of Zvi Ben Yosef the scribe and that the diary was indeed a gift from the Son of the Planets. Now I have understood that the scribe's son, in order to calm down the angry masses, wrote this scroll to protect his family after his father's death A surreptitious inner voice urged me, Get up! Find in Jerusalem the Tables of the Law, which are hidden there."

"Mr. D'Acosta, are you telling me that this diary can help in finding the Tables of the Law?" I asked with amazement.

"My friend Dan, you have to be patient. You probably understand, my friend, that, after I realized that the content of the diary is true, I devoted my time to investigate the strange signs in the diary. After putting a lot of effort into it, I finally managed to decode the great secret — the secret hiding place of the Tables of the Law. Now the manifest goal of my visit to the Old City of Jerusalem is disclosed to you."

"But we still do not know how you left the monastery, and you didn't tell us anything about the so many unsolved questions you had. What is this room in which we're now standing? Why did we fall in the water cistern and why did you register the location of that event as the Snake's Path? Is it possible to find the lost Tables of the Law after so many years?" I felt sure that Mr. D'Acosta had many more surprises in store for us."

Mr. D'Acosta gestured for us to wait. He went into the kitchen. After a few minutes, he came back with a tray loaded with goodies.

"Mr. D'Acosta, how did you manage to leave the monastery?" I started again, my mouth filled with food.

"Dear Dan!" He answered, "Don't rush; we have plenty of time. Please be patient and my great secret will be revealed to you.

"When I completed the translation of the diary, I believed that I had revealed the most hidden secret of the Jewish People. I realized that the papyrus the scribe's son wrote implied that his father, Zvi Ben Yosef the scribe, had disclosed to the Sons of Israel the secret hiding place of the Tables of the Law, but no one believed him. When the scribe had died, he was buried with his books, and the diary was never again seen by a living person.

"At that moment I took a vow to search for the Tables of the Law in order to expose them globally. From then on, my entire life was dedicated to searching for the Tables of the Law."

"What is this black ring? Where did you get it from?" I inquired while fidgeting around restlessly.

"Well, one day, while I was still at the monastery, I heard a voice calling my name. I raised my head and saw the old man, my acquaintance from the big library.'Mr. D'Acosta, get ready! You are about to go on a long journey within a short time. Go, take a bath, and change your robe!'

"When I was prepared, the old man took my hand in a commanding manner. We left my room and we crossed the big library on his way to his room. 'Are we about to go down to a new tunnel?' I asked my dignified companion.

"He darted a glance at me and said, 'Not to a tunnel, but rather to a new world!' Before he finished speaking, the floor started to sink quickly. *Where are we going now? To more secret rooms?* All at once the stone walls around us disappeared and I found myself passing through a cloud.

" 'A cloud?' I asked with amazement. 'Are we going to the bowels of the earth, or ascending high to the clouds?'

"I didn't even finish speaking and suddenly I saw something so contradictory to logic that I had to bite my hand to make sure I was not dreaming. From the incredibly fast sinking room floor, I could see the vastness of a land stretched below me. I asked myself in terrible confusion, *Is this an elevator or on an airplane?* Was I losing my sense of direction? Clouds, orchards, green fields ... *Where am I?*

"Then we slowed down, we ceased our dazzling flight, touching down at a big plaza that was surrounded by a spectacularly beautiful blossoming garden full of flowers. The splendid fragrance came to my nose. Confused I got off the floating floor and looked around. *Am I in the Garden of Eden? Is this heaven? Where am I and what could this magic be?*

" 'Mr. D'Acosta, follow my footsteps,' I heard my companion's voice. He took me by the hand again and pulled me gently in his wake. We left the garden of the flowers and walked through a boulevard of green bushes that gently swayed, like sea waves, in the mild wind. The picture was so tantalizing that I was afraid to wake up and find it was only a dream.

"We walked through the boulevard for a few moments until we arrived at trees that I had never seen before. They were as colorful as a rainbow — red, yellow, blue, white, purple – arrayed in an assortment of beautiful colors that were fused in a wonderful mixture.

"For a long time, I just passed through this land enchanted by the marvelous visage, until suddenly, I noticed, not far away from where I was, a large rectangular building sparkling like a shimmering diamond. For a moment I thought that it was just an optical illusion, but as I approached it, I perceived that it was indeed real.

" 'What is this building?' I asked my companion. But before I could complete my sentence, he just disappeared as if he was swallowed into it.

" 'Hey, what's going on? Am I dreaming? Where is the entrance?'

"I was still filled with amazement when I heard my companion's voice calling to me, 'Mr. D'Acosta, please enter the People's House. It is open on all of its sides.' I saw my companion's head peeking from the house and his smiling face and waving hand urged me to him. Cautiously and intrigued I stretched my arms forward and stepped ahead as if I was blind, toward the building. I was waiting for the expectable collision with its glistering wall. Most surprisingly I just crossed through its opaque walls without feeling any resistance. I stopped for a moment to examine what had just happened. I was amazed when I realized that I could see everything outside through the transparent walls.

"Knowing that I was unlikely to get answers to my many questions, I followed the footsteps of my companion who slowly climbed up a staircase. After a short climb, I saw a monolith black tablet hanged on the wall with tiny flickering lights on it. I looked closer and realized that it was a map of the Land of Israel. Next to the tiny spots of light, I could read the names of Hebrew settlements and on the top of the map, written in ancient Hebrew script, I could read: 'Map of the Land of Israel—2049. Next to it was the Jewish year—5809'. 'This is impossible! This was a map of Israel in the future because the year was only 5725. It will be 5809 in 84 years from now.' I called out.

" 'Yes, my young friend. This is a future map. You have been given the opportunity to see the future map of the Land of Israel.'

" 'But,' I asked, still amazed, 'what is this future map doing in this place?'

" 'Mr. D'Acosta, this is not the only surprise awaiting you in this place! You are about to have many more surprises, but only after the ceremony.'

" 'Ceremony? What kind of ceremony am I going to see?' I wondered whilst I was hastened to follow his footsteps.

" 'You are not going to see. You are going to be!' he answered laughing slightly.

"Next to a wide opening I saw a small sign on the wall and the inscription on it was in Hebrew: *Board of the Ten Tribes'*. A voice calling my name interrupted my thoughts. 'Mr. Arthur D'Acosta, please enter the hall of the Board.' I raised my head but did not see who was calling my name.

" 'Mr. D'Acosta, please come in. we are waiting for you, our young nephew!'

"All at once I was shaken from my thoughts, passed through the wide opening, and found myself standing on a stage, in front of a great silent crowd of people. I felt awkward in the face of such an unexpected welcome. The people there were wearing long white robes, and their shoes – I had never seen such odd-looking footwear before. Around a white table at the center of the stage sat the three Masters.

" 'Hello to you, Mr. Arthur D'Acosta,' the Spanish-speaking Master turned to me. 'Please come closer to our table.'

"I made my way nervously to the table of the Masters. When I arrived, he stood up, shook my hand, and greeted me in fluent Hebrew. His friend reached out to a golden box on the table, pulled out from it a green helmet, and placed it on my head. All of a sudden a wave of heat penetrated my head. My eyes were closed tightly when I heard a flow of many words in Hebrew running quickly into my dizzy head.

" 'Hello, Mr. Arthur D'Acosta. Welcome to the Land of the Ten Lost Tribes!' I heard the voice of the first Master. 'Your searches and efforts have borne fruits! Today the happiest day of your life has come. Finally, you have found the ten lost tribes, Arthur D'Acosta' He continued, 'You can see the well-known magic device that our scientist built many years ago. The *Information Accelerator* is capable of transferring into your head any information that you wish to have, a million times faster than the thinking of an average person. In just a few seconds you have fully learned the Hebrew language, and within a few hours, you could earn yourself a doctoral degree in the Hebrew language. And now, Mr. D'Acosta, take up the gauntlet and tell to these dignitaries of the ten lost tribes in your newly-acquired Hebrew your life story.'

"For a little over an hour, I told them my story and also the concealed secret of my family; that I was a descendent of the Marranos. The elders of the tribes listened to my story attentively. When I had finished they stood up and stayed like that in silence for a long time.

" 'Mr. D'Acosta,' the Master said, 'we honor you for your sincere words!'

" 'And how do you know that I am not lying?' I responded.

" 'Look up, can you see the white ball hanging up in the center of the hall? This ball is called the truth-light. Whenever a mild lie is being told, the ball would change its color; whenever a severe lie is being told, it would turn black and emits a sharp whistle. The ball remained snow-white throughout, indicating that everything you said is true'

" 'Unbelievable!' I said with excitement. 'I have truly found the ten lost tribes!'

" 'Unfortunately, your story of this great discovery must not be disclosed. You ought to keep this secret and many others concealed in your heart, never to share them with anyone, till your last day,' another of the Masters said.

" 'And now,' the eldest of the Masters added, 'our lost countryman, please wear this ring on your finger.' It was the black ring."

Chapter 15

Four Thousand Years of History

"The moment I placed the ring on my finger, one of the Masters stood up, and addressed the audience:

This is a special day. We are meeting with for the first time someone whose family has been following Jewish tradition secretly because they feared the surrounding hostility, and now for the first time, he is endowed with the opportunity to meet his long-lost people. I'm a descendant of the last enthroned Israelite dynasty. Four thousand years ago Abraham, the founder of the Jewish nation, left his home at Ur-Cassdim between the Pratt and Hidekel Rivers[11].

After many years of settling in the new land, namely, the Land of Israel, some years of drought in the Land of Israel forced his descendants' Jacob and his sons, to go to the wealthy

---

[11] Pratt and Hidekel are the Hebrew names for the Euphrates and Tigris, where Ur of the Chaldees (Ur Kasdim) sits

Kingdom of Egypt. It was not before long that the Israelites were put into slavery, and built the pyramids there. Another four hundred years of slavery had passed, and the Israelites, led by their great leader Moshe Ben Amram, managed to be released from their plight. On their way back to the Land of Israel they were given the Torah of Moshe, and thus they became the first nation to believe in one abstract impalpable God.

Their journey back to their land had them fight with many tribes that resisted them as they conquered the Promised Land again. The twelve tribes had left Egypt and resettled again in every region of the country. After a long settling period without a ruler, the twelve tribes decided to have a king. This is how Saul Ben Kish became the first king, but he and his son Yehonatan were killed in the war against the Sea Peoples invading from neighboring lands.

Then Saul's son, Ish-bosheth was enthroned. However, two years later, this second king was murdered and usurped by David the son of Jesse. This wise and daring third king eventually defeated the Sea People.

King David freed the land of Israel from the yokes of the invaders and from their plundering and usurping manners. He then expanded his conquests way beyond Hama, next to Damascus. Next, he conquered Jerusalem and turned it into the infinite capital of the Land of Israel. This was about 1,000 BCE. After King David's death, his son King Solomon, the fourth king of Israel, was enthroned and was renowned for his wisdom. He built the First Temple and built and strengthened the town. His son succeeded him but his kingdom didn't last for long and shortly after that the people of Israel were divided into two separate factions.

The ten tribes enthroned Jeroboam son of Nebat as their ruler while the tribes of Benjamin and Judah were against him. Thus, two separate kingdoms were created in the Land of Israel: the Kingdom of Judea with Jerusalem as its capital, and the Kingdom of Israel with the ancient city of Samaria as its capital. These two kingdoms fought against one another many times. About two hundred years after that in 733 BCE the Kingdom of Israel was conquered by a ruthless Assyrian invader and the majority of its inhabitants were exiled to Assyria.

After several years, the Assyrians invaded the land again and crushed the remnants. Thus no one knows where the sons of the ten lost tribes had gone and what happened to them. And now, our young brother, Arthur D'Acosta you are the first man to know where the descendants of ten lost tribes had settled down.

And now, I'm going to unveil to you the fate and history of the ten lost tribes from the beginning of their exile to this very day at their hidden under-terrestrial country, which was built deep in the bowels of the earth.

"The words of the Master seemed to me like a legend and filled me with excitement which I had to subdue and then I just listened attentively as he continued. The Master still standing, examined the crowd of people around him, and continued:

As you have heard already, the Kingdom of Israel was conquered twice. Most of its land was conquered during the first invasion, and in the second invasion, the tremendously fortified capital, Samaria, fell while the remnants of the ten tribes were exiled.

The exile of the Sons of Israel to Assyria started as a strenuous journey For many months they marched on difficult paths, climbed high mountains, and crossed arid and desolated deserts. It was during summer and the days were extremely hot and the paucity of food and water took its high toll on their way. On many occasions, young girls were kidnapped from the lined-up flock by the Assyrian soldiers and ransomed only by high forfeit or were abducted and vanquished forever.

During the first days of the march, a number of families dared to escape at the deep of night, but, if they were caught, they were viciously murdered in front of the eyes of their countrymen. This deterred most of them who didn't have any other choice and had to continue to march despite their hardship and great suffering.

After many months of an exhausting journey, the Israelites arrived in the enemy's country, Assyria, in a state of exhaustion and weariness. They were then divided into three groups. The first group was put to work in the fields but was eventually sent to build the new capital city of the enemy, Dur-Sharrukin. The second one was sent to build the city of Havur, located in the mountains on the border between Persia and Assyria. The third group, which was not capable of hard labor, was sent far away beyond Assyria to the mountainous country on the other side of the Gozan River in Afghanistan.

When the first group was removed from the fields and sent to build the new capital city, they set down in a large city of tents together with many other tribes that were also conquered by the Assyrians and were exiled as slaves. The Sons of Israel suffered many attacks from thieves and robbers from neighboring tribes. Their complaints to the Assyrian military commanders were ignored. No one listened to them. They managed to secure a few months free from attacks only by bribing their Assyrian ruler. However, this period of grace ended and the robberies started again, even during daylight every single day to the horrible terror and cry of the desolated people.

In light of this, the leaders of the camp gathered together, and quickly they enlisted a policing force from the Sons of Israel. After many bids and bribery, the Assyrian ruler was willing to sell them a small number of daggers, swords, and shields. The armed policing guardsmen were arrayed to protect the camp, and soon the robbers' attacks were stopped, and the peace returned to the camp.

After hard eight years of strenuous work in building the capital, some happy tidings have arrived – the Assyrian king had died. But their joy did not last long. The heir to the throne was even worse than his father, and the life of the Sons of Israel became even more difficult and bitter.

'I want you to build a city manifold larger and stronger than the one you built in Samaria or this one you were building here,' the Assyrian king said to the Sons of Israel.

'We are back to our Egyptian days of slavery and subjugation! Is there any place in this world which is secured from the oppressiveness of man?' the Israelites screamed in great despair.

'Why shouldn't we escape from this land and live like wildlife in caves, gorges, and underneath the ground?' a young man called out with great excitement to the people.

His suggestion resulted in thundering laughter and for a moment, they forgot their deep suffering and despair. 'Good-looking young man, we want to live on the face of the earth, not underneath it,' they answered him.

'A day will come and you will kneel down before me,' the young man called at them angrily.

There came three more difficult years of strenuous and wearing-out work. One day a rumor was passed in the camps of the subjugated peoples that the Assyrian King had been wounded in battle and they began to relish with joy. 'This is the end of the rule of evilness,' they shouted loudly.

On that same day, the elders of the people climbed up a prominent hill and the entire camp of Israelites surrounded them down below. 'We have gone through three difficult years, and now we shall do what our ancestors did in Egypt. The king is wounded and his army is defeated. This is the right time to escape this damned place,' the elders claimed aloud. 'Get ready to leave!'

Three days later, as the last rays of sunset faded, long caravans headed stealthily to the nearby mountains.

Stealthy messengers hurried to the city of Habor. They helped their brothers get ready for the great journey. The two groups met in the eastern part of the city and marched quickly eastward. In a hasty pace, they arrived at the banks of Lake Urmia, a Bitter Lake in the North of Iran. When the fleeing people saw that no one was chasing them, they felt reassured and stayed on the banks of the lake for three days. After having regaining their energy and rearranging their columns they continued on their way to the mountains that surround the Caspian Sea. These mountains are called the Dagh Chufuty, which means 'Mountain of the Highland Jews' to this very day.

Twenty years after being exiled from their country, the Sons of Israel had found peace and quiet in immensely remote mountains far away from their own country and started a new chapter in their lives. Through for many days, messengers kept searching for the third exiled group of the Israelites, but they could not find any trace of their lost brothers.

The years went by peacefully and the people forgot the sufferings of their past. Peace was restored, in those desolate and far mountains. Multiple herds of sheep and cattle filled the mountains, and the land became green and yielded the produce of the earth. However, this ideal scene ended as a thunderstorm arrives on a clear day, when vandalistic tribes invaded the camp, leaving much devastation behind them. Many homes were ruined, plundered, set on fire and many people were killed. Girls were kidnapped and were never returned. Herds of sheep and cattle were looted, while the remaining people sank into shock and despair. For many long days, they sat and mourned. 'There is no place in this world where one can be secured from the cruelty of human beasts!' they said with bitter despair.

Among the crowd of mourning people was the young man, who now has matured to become a man, that one who had called the people to join him to live in caves, and hide in the bowels of the earth. Now he stood up and called to his people, 'My brothers, Sons of Israel! If you are awaiting life come and follow me! Within thirty days, my family and I are going to abandon this wretched place and walk toward the Great Cave in the Land of the Black Mountains.'

Twenty days later the man, named Netzah Ben Israel, stood at the center of the camp, and summoned the people again, 'In ten days my family and I are going out to the Great Cave in the Land of the Black Mountains that touch the sky. If you are awaiting life follow us!'

'Where is the Land of the Black Mountains that touch the sky?' the crowd of people asked.

'All of you know that I am a shepherd and that I know all the paths that lead up to the horizon, to the Great Salt Desert, the Khwar Desert in Iran. A while ago, I wandered with my herd in search of pasture, and suddenly I saw a wild man coming from the Black Mountains. We quickly became friends and sat to eat together.'

'The wild man told me that he met a people whom he called Tetim who looked a lot like me. Before we departed he handed me a map and warned me to enter the Great Cave with warm wool clothing. For many days I kept our meeting in secret, but now the day has come and I and my family are going to climb to that place. If you wish to follow my footsteps prepare wool clothing because it is very cold in this land. The peaks of the mountains are blanketed by clouds.'

'Is it possible to have a cave that can shelter the entire population of our people? Is this cave is a figment of your imagination or the product of your strange dreams?' said the pranksters of the people and broke up into laughter.

For a moment Netzah Ben Israel froze and then he lifted his hand and replied, 'Just a few days ago, you buried your dead and claimed that there is no place for you on the face of the earth to be secured of the cruelty of the human beast! And now, where are you aiming at?'

'He is speaking the truth!' declared many of the audience that surrounded him. 'There is no shelter for us from many the cruelty of the human beast! We will follow your footsteps to the Land of the high mountains!'

The time passed quickly and long caravans of the people started to follow the footsteps of the shepherd Netzah Ben Israel. Only a few of the people did not follow including those who were not fit enough to endure the obstacles and hardships and they were therefore left to their destinies. To this day, no one knows what happened to them.

At the beginning of the month of Nisan, the Israelites embarked on their long journey to the Great Cave at the land of the Black Mountains. At the head of the caravan was the dreamer once a supple boy now a man and a leader. The long convoy made its way in the direction of the bitter lake that they had formerly passed during their escape from slavery in Assyria. They then turned eastward and marched along the feet of the mountains that encircled the Great Salt Desert. Because of teeming brigands who robbed along the main road, they followed the peripheral edge of the desert away from the main path.

The journey along the peripheral salt desert was strenuous. Many times they had to face attacks of dangerous beasts, which came from the mountains. On their long journey, they passed many blue lakes and rivers, but their salty water was non-potable. The people yelled from thirst, 'why did we come to die in this desert? Our situation might have been better if we were prisoners and not destined to die in this terrible place!'

'A bunch of stupid cowards!' cried Netzah Ben Israel. 'Your forefathers when they left Egypt after four-hundreds years of slavery, also grumbled and lamented about the bitter hardship in their way, and you know well what befell them. You just want to descend to that same level of our ancestors during their exodus from Egypt.' When the people heard his reproach they started to refrain from complaints and dared not to moan about it anymore. From that day on, they walked silently like a caravan of ghosts.

In five months the Sons of Israel had crossed the Great Salt Desert and arrived at the highlands in Afghanistan. Cold winds came from the mountains; the temperate, nice autumn days were replaced by the cold and darkness. Now they accelerated their pace, searching for shelter to hide from the pending winter. Following an exhausting voyage, they reached the Great River, the Lamand River in Afghanistan. As soon as they reached the Great River, they immediately started to prepare for winter, which had already welcomed them with strong rain and stormy winds. As they completed to spread their large wool tents and strengthened the spikes the storm was strengthening and hail started to storm the green sheets. When they were still hiding from the stormy wheater, suddenly came the alarming voice of their watchman that announced the danger of approaching enemies. The men were quickly arrayed with their arms and deployed in posts around the camp. Three large groups of horsemen appeared on top of the surrounding mountains. They were riding rapidly toward the camp.

When they were within a few hundred yards, the horsemen stopped and sent a messenger to the camp.

'Who are you and what are you looking for in our country?' the messenger used the Median language to ask. 'Go back to your own country. Otherwise, we will start a war against you within three days!'

'We are members of a sad and bitter nation. Because of the cruelty of humans, we were uprooted from our good land, and we became vagabonds in this world. We are now making our way to the land of the high celestial mountains, the Black Mountains.'

'From where were you uprooted, and who is your God?' the messenger asked.

'We were uprooted from the Land of Israel, the land of milk and honey that we bequeathed from the God of Abraham, Isaac, and Jacob.'

Before even completing this sentence the enemy's messenger burst into cries of joy. He stormed into the camp yelling loudly, 'I am your brother Ben Israel and so are all the horsemen around me!'

When the horsemen heard the messenger's words, they went down from their horses and hurried to meet their brothers who were in utter bewilderment. There were not enough words to express the joyous meeting of the three exiled groups after they were separated for so long by the Assyrian Empire. Even the strong biting winds stopped in the face of such a passionate and exciting reunion. The Sons of Israel continued up the river in their way toward the settlement of their lost brothers.

They arrived there two days later, with their own people who rushed to welcome them with songs and dances. The skies suddenly became clear, making the joy even greater. This kind of happiness had not been seen for many years. Who could possibly believe that the day would come when all the members of the Ten Tribes would meet in this remote place?

They passed the hardship of the stormy days of winter with joy and then came spring. Soon tiny almond buds started to blossom and the white coat of snow disappeared.

On one such spring day, Netzah Ben Israel arrived at the center of the camp and called out loud, 'Brothers! I am tired of life wandering and fleeing away. I have a dream – to live far-far away from the cruelty of the human beast. Even here, in the land of many mountains, we are not protected from the evilness of humans. In a few days, I am going to get to the Great Cave'.

His words have stirred many people at the camp. Six weeks later, approximately twenty-five thousand people gathered at the entrance to the camp, bringing with them great supplies of food and herds of sheep, ready to set off in their journey to the Great Cave. The parting was heartbreaking and they vowed to meet again.

One-tenth of the people took it to follow the footsteps of Netzah Ben Israel onward. The camp dwellers sent two battalions of horsemen, armed and ready to protect the people who went to the Land of the Black Mountains in today's Kashmir. The group of people marched slowly on the winding road through the high mountains, the deep valleys, and the narrow gorges

They have been on the road for four months when they reached the Great Valley, the Kabul Valley in Afghanistan. After a short touching ceremony, they departed from their brothers, the horsemen who accompanied them, and continued on their way. Despite their weariness, they were inspired with energy to complete their journey.

After three more months, they arrived at the land where the mountains touch the sky, the Karakoram Mountains. They stood on these high mountains all thrilled for a long time and feasted their eyes on the beautiful view. Even in their wildest dreams, they could have not imagined anywhere so beautiful.

Then they set out their camp near a brook and rushed to find wood for the winter that began sooner than they had expected. Netzah Ben Israel accompanied by ten trackers left urgently in a search of the shorter path to the Great Cave. As soon as they left the camp, a blizzard started and hit everything forcefully, blanketing the land and paths with a white magical coat. This mighty storm had scared some of his companions, the trackers, who stood up and demanded,

'Where are we going to?' they said beaten by their mental affliction. 'Why must we die in this white desert?'

'This is not the right time to lament and cry from fear. Remember that we are here to find a hiding place for the people. Get up and follow me. Would you like to return with empty hands to the people and tell them that you were scared by some snow and intense winds? Look, here is the map of the land. Tomorrow at dawn we will arrive at the Great Cave'.

When they heard the reproach of their leader, they were overwhelmed with embarrassment and shame. Then they stood up and declared, 'We shall follow your footsteps wherever you go.'

Then the trackers jumped on their feet and started to march without taking any rest until sundown. They then found a small niche that kept them away from the snow. At sunrise, they hurriedly set off. After a long hike, they saw a big mountain with three peaks.

When Netzah Ben Israel saw the mountain, he stopped on spot, marked a large circle with his hiking pole on the ground, and crossed it into four equal parts, stuck his pole on the right half, and started to walk forward. After three thousand steps he turned right and fastened his pace while the ten trackers hurried after him. After a short walk in a deep stream, they reached a small lake continued to walk through it to a grove of wide-trunk trees. Pointing out the trees Netzah Ben Israel stated, 'The Great Cave is located behind this grove'.

The trackers followed him and soon the opening of the cave was revealed. It's hard to express the amount of joy Netzah Ben Israel and his companions had. With their yells of hooray and joy, they congratulated their leader. Then they all nimbly lit some torches they prepared beforehand and entered the Great Cave. It took them one walking hour in each direction to across the cave, and they measured each distance at about five thousand meters.

Their joy increased when they realized that the very low temperatures outside did not prevail inside of the cave to the extent that they had to remove their sheepskin coats. They started to examine the surface of the cave and searched thoroughly for more niches and tunnels that may lead to the heart of the mountain.

The delight with which the people that stayed at the camp congratulated them when they arrived back was enormous and many of them started to dance and jitter in rumbling elation in the showering rain. The next day at dawn they started the hectic effort of packing and folding down their tents and belongings. Soon they all joined together in one crowd of people that set off to the cave. After three days of hiking, they arrived at the Great Cave. In a short period of time, the surface of the cave was totally changed. The Israelites divided the cave equally among all the people. They even opened some more narrow paths so that daylight could break in and illuminate the cave.

Their youth began to explore the long and narrow burrows and tunnels that were never before explored by humans.

During the second month following their arrival at the cave, something terrible happened that left the entire flock at the camp shocked. A group of youngsters disappeared into one of the long tunnels and had not returned after three nerve-wracking days.

'We must go to search for the boys right now' decreed their leaders; indeed urgently the troop of trackers led by Netzah Ben Israel set off to follow and track the young boys' footsteps that led to one of the tunnels.

Chapter 16

The Land of Dreams

The trackers passed through the winding tunnels for many days. Occasionally they stopped in place, blew their ram's horns, and listened carefully to hear a reply. For three weeks they found nothing. A disturbing silence pervaded the camp as neither the lost sons nor the trackers returned. 'The cave is doomed,' people started to whisper. The despair culminated in a cry of anguish. 'Maybe they had no more food? Maybe there was no more oil in their lamps, and they are now fumbling their way in the dark with no hope? What fate awaits them? What fate awaits us?'

A larger mission started to get organized for the search when they heard some subdued voices coming from the center of the mountain. The people froze tantalized and waited, breathless. Then they heard loud, happy cries of joy coming up from the scouts and they saw a long convoy with torches that emerged from the bowels of the mountain and marched straight toward the camp.

'We've found the Garden of Eden! We've found the Garden of Eden!' they heard the voices coming closer and their cries of joy strengthened as they saw their group of youngsters returning behind the trackers.

After everyone was calmed down, all of the residents at the camp gathered to listen to the trackers' story:

'For an entire week, we were fumbling around tracking through the endlessly forking tunnels. We became weaker and weaker and our reservoir of candle oil was almost finished. Our exhaustion and fatigue encumbered heavily on our pace until we stood still in place, lacking any further motivation to continue. After deliberations, we resumed our venturing into the unknown. For three more days we advanced thus with renewed energies. Our last jar of oil was almost finished and only one torch was left to light our way.

'We walked and walked and walked. Finally, we sat down, exhausted. There was no oil left in the jars. Fear started to creep into our hearts; our weariness and exhaustion only increased. Despite our fatigue, we stood up and walked slowly even further into the unknown. The fire of the last torch was slowly dying out, portending the story of its final extinguishment, conveying to us a clue of cruel fate. There was total darkness around us. We were overwhelmed by strong feelings of fear and confusion. We continued straight ahead! We must find our sons!' we encouraged each other with loud calls and continued like blind people, walking hand in hand in silence in the dark.

'We walked like that in the darkness for an unknown period of time when suddenly the leader at the head stopped and pointed to a tiny spot of light far away. At first, we thought that were some optical illusions because of the darkness, but as we came closer to it we saw the tiny spot of light grow until we met with the light of day. At first, we assumed it was the light coming from our camp. There are no words to express our surprise when we came closer to a wide crater and realized the vegetation that thrived at the foot of its slopes. We saw many types of plants and fruit trees that were unfamiliar to us. At the center of the crater, we discovered a lake of warm, clear water. Wild animals filled every corner of it.

'How come, such lush vegetation and a lake of hot water exist during the freezing cold of winter? 'We have arrived at the

Garden of Eden,' we exclaimed with excitement. For a moment, while we scouted this paradise, we just forgot everything about the mission that had brought us there. But there are no words on earth to express our joy when we saw our lost youngsters wading in the lake. It was difficult to convince them to return with us to their warring families.'

'Can such a wonderful place like that possibly exist?' the camp people asked their youngsters.

'Look, you can see it with your own eyes!' The youngsters took out from their bags the overgrown, beautiful fruits and presented them to the crowd.

'They speak the truth,' the trackers confirmed. 'If we had not seen it with our own eyes, we would not have believed it.'

The story of the young boys persuaded the entire inhabitants of the camp. They all jumped with excitement and quickly started to pack up their belongings and gather their herds. Soon a long convoy was gathered to set off immersed with joy towards the new Garden of Eden.

The Sons of Israel were confronted with a new way of life upon their arrival at the green crater, which was surrounded by steep mountains that soared up to the sky. The dwellers of the camp called this new era the Shell Days. For a long time, they have lived disconnected from the world outside and they knew nothing about it after they had sealed the opening of the tunnel and thus they had stayed concealed from the outside world.

"The Master ceased the flow of his storytelling, took a long sip of water, cleared his throat, and continued his story:

For many years they had been freed from any worries; the fruit trees having great yields and the herds of sheep multiplied in abundance. The bees too took part and contributed their sweet blessing. The dream of the people to be released from their fears of the cruelty of the human beast had come true. As time went by, their numbers multiplied greatly and therefore they started to dig into the bowels of the earth and curved into the crater walls in order to increase the size of their dreamland. However, about two hundred years after they arrived at the crater, the cave diggers could no longer provide for the needs of the growing population. This difficult situation forced them to search hectically for new solutions. They soon came up with new inventions that made the diggers' work easier, and a new generation of students and researchers started to flourish.

You may not believe my story that hundreds of years before the time of Christ, during darker times while nations around the world were viciously fighting one another, the Israelites were already starting their research in physics and mathematics. Approximately one hundred and fifty more years went by, and they were captivated by a choking feeling and felt trapped. Many of them wanted to get out of the crater and go up to the surface of the earth.

But before anyone took that step, an amazing breakthrough had affected everyone's lives – the invention of the 'Dig-Light' by a genius youth named Ben Uri Israel. It was a strange-looking metal monster with many glass eyes. When it was placed in the sun, shortly after switching on its engine some smoke and fire then were emitted from rocks, until they were suddenly melting as if they were made of wax. The invention of the dig-light enabled the people to go deeper far into the bowels of the mountain and expand vastly their narrow territory far beyond their dreams. The genius youth, Ben Uri, helped lead the people to unimaginable breakthroughs and awe-inspiring achievements.

Another miraculous invention was developed twenty years later by Ben Uri Israel that was called the 'Store-Light', an amazing device that would be recharged by daylight for three days and then used to light up an entire cave for a couple of years. The unlimited source of light allowed them to venture with their plantations deep into the bowels of the earth. The vegetation just thrived, blossomed, and yielded an abundance, a great amount of produce.

Obviously, since the invention of the Store-Light, this unique magical wonder was enhanced further, and currently, it doesn't call for long periods of recharging while its capacity has been expanded to provide many more years of daylight. Time has passed by and brought many changes to the ten tribes: they grew exponentially in numbers and they no longer live in the Great Crater.

" 'What?' I exclaimed, surprised, and terminating the Master's story. 'Do you mean to tell me that—'

" 'Yes, the Ten Tribes have incredibly deepened their advancement into the center of this mountainous range and today they are dwelling in sumptuous cities hundreds of meters underneath the highest summits of the world.'

" 'If it is so, to where did you arrive?' I hurried to ask the Master to whose story about the fate of the ten lost tribes I listened to long on the stage. I inquired, 'If I am in the crater right now, then how is it possible to have in front of my eyes all these green fields, streams, groves, and above all, the bright sky? Is it possible to see a bright sky deep in the bowels of a mountain?'

"Sounds of laughter were heard in the audience, causing me to blush. The Master then explained, 'Well dear brother, the beautiful blue sky is merely a very sizeable Store-Light that illuminates up the cave ceiling in blue light and creates the impression that there is a sky here. This wonderful light does wonders in the agriculture of our plants, trees, and much of the produce that comes from our fields.'

"Then he continued, 'Arthur D'Acosta, our dear brother! The entire network of caves and niches, which you had been exploring for many days is part of the place in which our ancestors settled when they first arrived at the Great Cave. After many years of moving far deeper and beyond the mountain range we went back to reclaim the cavern and today it is unrecognizably transformed. This is how the vast barren cavern had turned into a land of groves, streams, and green fields. We occasionally go there and show the place to our children. This is why the place is lit and thrives like the Garden of Eden.'

" 'And now, please excuse me for barraging you with many questions but please tell me about the bizarre monastery that I have lived in since I first arrived here? And why did you accept me into your secret place even though you knew nothing about who I was and what were my intentions?'

" 'The large complex above the ground, which is called the Bewitched Monastery by the locals, is actually a very advanced observatory and the silent monks are actually our brothers, the scientists who research the planets. Since we were concerned about our neighbors, the tribes around us, we have spread many stories about the Black Mountains, the Karakoram Mountains, that they are the dwelling place of gods and thus human beings are prohibited to climb there. However, a visitor to the monastery would not even notice that actually, it is an observatory since we had camouflaged it in order to deter random passers-by. If someone would get closer to the observatory they will meet with a show that would never be forgotten. You too had a very interesting meeting with the humanoid gorilla near the observatory. His job is to get rid of unwanted visitors who get near the observatory.'

" 'What?' I was amazed. 'The monkey man assists the people in the observatory?'

" 'This is correct. The humanoid gorilla was created in the laboratory of the scientists of the ten lost tribes,' he confirmed again.

" 'So why didn't you drive me away when I arrived at the observatory and climbed on it? You had no idea who I was and what my intentions were.'

"I heard sounds of laughter among the audience."

" 'Why not? After all, we got to know you well before you had arrived there.'

" 'You got to know me? How could that possibly be?' I asked amazed.

" 'We used an unusual device called a *Head-Recorder*. We know all the mental stuff that passed in your head from birth till now. This exquisite copying device has visual and audio features and can present your entire life in images and the utterances that you said. When you arrived at the observatory we already knew everything about your past, your fears, and your concealed family secret.'

" 'Really?! That sounds magnificent!' I was amazed by this new revelation. 'And how are new books and magazines supplied so quickly to such a remote place?'

" 'You see, we have an enormous global network of underground tunnels that we have dug over the centuries. We can arrive immediately and swiftly to just about anywhere on earth. One such tunnel leads to our fatherland, the Land of Israel. We can move inside these tunnels very quickly from one place to another without any fear or difficulty.'

" 'Are you saying that you built fast trains to traverse these long tunnels?' I interjected.

" 'No, my young friend, we did not build any trains, cars or jets. You will find out about this too shortly. After you learn how to use the tunnels, you will be able to go from this place and even go back to your father's home. No one will stop you. However, if you wish to live with your nation, here in the hidden country, we would be happy to have you as a brother. Here you will no longer need to live like the Marranos. Here you will be safe from the insane people and human animals that exist across the entire universe.'

" 'For thousands of years, we have anxiously watched our brothers who were left on the surface. We have seen the actions of the human beasts that have chased them all over the world. We see the ignorance of the masses, marching after vicious and insane leaders. We have seen all the atrocities that the members of our nation have gone through over the generations when no one came to their aid. We saw the ignorance of the masses marching after strange people claiming to save the world and the people from their problems. The world saviors have done nothing … human beasts are walking around free doing whatever they wish. These human beasts have become rulers occasionally and the world watched in silence.'

" 'This is why we remain deep inside the earth. However, we know that the day will come when the human beasts will disappear from the face of the earth and people will no longer be interested in tyranny and power,' the elder of the three Masters told me."

"This is my entire story, my dear friends. Now you know how I arrived at Masada through the tunnels, and you obviously understand now why I avoided meeting you."

Chapter 17

The Prisoner from Space

"Mr. D'Acosta," I said, "I have one minor request before we depart. Please tell us how the Sons of Israel managed to dig underground tunnels throughout the entire world, including under the oceans."

D'Acosta took a glass of water from the table across from him and emptied it in a single long gulp. He took a deep breath, looked at the ceiling, and closed his eyes.

He was quiet for a long moment. "Well, my curious friend," he broke the silence, "I am going to tell you the last one; after that, I will say no more. My last story is about the Son of the Planets who was captured by the ten tribes."

"What?" I jumped on my feet as if I was electrified. "The Son of the Planets was captured by the Sons of Israel?"

D'Acosta was surprised by my great excitement but continued with his story. "My story about the capturing of the Son of the Planets will shake the entire knowledge you have in physics and will seem like a fairytale to you. It's the secret of the Son of the Planets that arrived here from some unknown worlds. I have already told you that my greatest dream, to find the remnants of the ten lost tribes, has been fulfilled and I met them in a world that was, to me, captivating and fantastic. I have learned of their many amazing inventions and about the extent of their achievements, most of which are still are unknown to me. I believe that the day will come when you will witness this great marvel underneath the ground. At the times when peoples chose outrageously crazy things — wars, murder, and robbery — scientists of the ten tribes were already making great advances in the bowels of the earth."

"I had two pieces of evidence about the emergence of the Son of the Planets. The first one was the scroll that reported about the strange thing that the Sons of Israel saw a few days after their arrival at the Great Cave. This scroll also includes the story of the spy David Ben David, who explored the land of elephants. David Ben David tells about the strange sight of the appearance of the carriage in the sky, the descending of God to earth, and his ascending back there after forty days. You might be aware that when people saw the cosmic vessel, the Mindneron, and the Son of the Planets descending from it in his weird attire they couldn't comprehend it."

"The second piece of evidence, which is already familiar to you, is the diary of the scribe Zvi Ben Yosef."

"I have only one book of the three that were communicated by the Son of the Planets to the scribe Zvi Ben Yosef, which is the notorious diary. I kept looking for the other two books for a long time, but I could not find them. Whilst I was searching for these books, I also spent many hours at the library. One day I discovered an incredible book that unfolds the story of the Diaspora of the Sons of Israel from their exile to Assyria almost up the present day."

"On one page there was a detailed answer to your question on how it's possible to dig such long tunnel in the bowels of the earth and underneath the oceans. These tunnels were first dug after Moshe Ben Rechasim invented the Drill of the String Light, which could drill immensely big holes into the depths of the mountain and only had to be recharged once every hundred years by the sun rays. It can dig through great distances while staying in subterranean mode."

"While reading about the light drill I also found a description of the capture of the Son of the Planets, who was hurt by this machine."

"This event happened one summer a thousand years ago. An alarm went off, signaling danger. A scout used the public address system that a figure was floating above the observatory on the monastery."

" 'This is impossible!' the scientists at the observatory claimed. 'There is no human being on Earth who knows how to hover.'

" 'Could it be an angel?' asked the guard.

" 'There are angels only in fairy tales. Any child knows this simple truth,' the scientists answered.

" 'But why is he spying on us? Maybe it is a spying angel,' asked the chief scientist in humor. 'Why would God need spies or angels? Can't he see our actions clearly at any He wants?'

" 'We will soon know all about him,' the chief scientist said. Then the scientists directed the light drill toward the hovering figure, shooting its high-intensity light. To the great surprise of the scientists, the figure started to twist and turn as if injured and descend until it slowly reached the ground near the observatory.

" 'This is unbelievable!' exclaimed the chief scientist. 'The light drill can melt huge rocks, but this being stayed intact. I have never seen anything which can withstand the light drill.'

"The scientists went out to the landing site of the hovering being. They approached cautiously, shielded behind the light drill, prepared for any new surprise. The Being lay motionless on a big rock and they thought it was dead. After a long examination with a headscanner, the chief scientist concluded, 'This is strange. There are no signs that the figure was hurt. The body is dead but the head is alive!'

"The Being was brought to the central scientific institute, where it became a major topic for research. Alive or dead? A human being or a superior being? It became a thorny question and endless debates and words were spilled over the fantastic Being they have captured. Neither a body of an animal nor of a human being! claimed one group. The other one claimed that its exceptional body was a natural mutation. The entire set of experiments was inconclusive. The scientists eventually decided to place the Being into a large stove and see its reaction to heat.

" 'If the huge light drill did not kill this Being, nothing ever will!' said the chief scientist.

"The scientists placed the strange Being in an extremely powerful stove. Surging flames engulfed the Being. For a moment, they all believed that it had been totally burned to ashes. But it did not disappear. They fed the fire for a month, and yet the Son of the Planets stayed intact. 'Make the fire stronger, up to its highest intensity!' the chief scientist ordered.

"Three months later, the scientists peeked again into the hot stove. They were amazed to see that the Son of the Planets absorbed the heat of the stove and that his body turned white like hot iron. Then the flames suddenly died out as the stove was turned off. 'It just moved!' the scientists said, frightened. They were paralyzed with fear when the body of the Son of the Planets started alternately shrinking and stretching. He then stretched to his full length, rolled over to one side, and hovered to stand on what appeared to be his feet.

" 'Quick! Bring the light drill!' the chief scientist yelled. His aides directed the light drill toward the Being in the stove and fired with its fullest intensity. Sparks of violet, green and red light beams were seen emerging from the Son of the Planets' body, blinding the scientists for several moments.

"When the intensive radiation stopped, the scientists saw the Son of the Planets floating out through the stove wall. Petrified like salt pillars they watched the amazing sight. The Son of the Planets floated above the stove hovering slowly and lower in the direction of the frozen scientists. Then he started to transmit his words into their heads, 'Do not be afraid! I do not have any bad intentions and I am not interested in any revenge. All I want is to get to know you better and learn about your lifestyle.'

" 'Who are you?' the chief scientist asked after recovering from his shock, 'And what do you want?'

"I am neither a god nor an angel. I am a citizen of an immensely distant planet. My home planet is located at the Light Triangle in the Seventh Sky.'

" 'How is it possible? How did you arrive here and why did you hover above the monastery?'

"The Son of the Planets transmitted his story about the Light Triangle and his interesting journeys in the universes of outer space. He even told them how the Mindneron had crashed and tumbled down to the Land of Elephants. 'Since the crash of the spaceship I have been touring your world, continually investigating it. I visited your ancestors after their arrival at the Great Cave but doubted whether they would survive there. I must say that I was very impressed by the secret observatory which is hidden inside the monastery. But the greatest wonder is the world that you have built under the highest peaks on your planet. I was surprised to see such an advanced thing on such a backward planet. The greatest surprise of all was the light drill. I was so surprised by it that I did not activate a shielding screen that protects me against radiation such as that of the light drill.'

" 'The light drill deactivated the center of strength in my body until I could hardly land. I was fortunate that you placed me inside the stove. The intense heat has recharged my body.'

" 'With your permission, I would like to stay here for a few days and then to resume my travels through your tiny world. In gratitude for your willingness to have me, I will leave some priceless gifts with you.'

"The Son of the Planets left many formulas that helped in building some very sophisticated machines as well as to improve the light drill that built the entire network of worldwide tunnels. A short time after his departure, there was an onset of new inventions and discoveries in the land of the ten lost tribes.

"During the time when the Son of the Planets spent with the ten lost tribes, he talked about other beliefs on distant planets he had met during his tours there, and those of our planet. Here is his story:

> I have been to all the Seven Skies and many different fantastic planets. I saw unfamiliar animals and unique human beings. In the same manner as your own planet, across the Seven Worlds, there were also all sorts of rituals that have developed there.
>
> When I visited the Green Planet in the Third Sky at the beginning of its development, I saw how worshiping had begun, and it happened in the same way as it was developed on your own planet.

The inception of beliefs started from the cultivation of land by ancient men. During the period of sowing, sacrifices of human beings were offered to the gods by the farmers.

These terrible rituals have spread over many planets. The primordial man tried to give explanations to unexplained and fearsome natural phenomena, such as darkness, light, bolts of lightning, thunder, floods, earthquakes that scared him and motivated him to search for ways to please those great, extraordinary powers. As early as prehistoric times, ancient man started to try compromising with those natural forces such as darkness, light, lightning, thunder, floods, and many other things by worshipping them. With the evolution of man, hosts of priests and magicians emerged, and they vouched for their special knowledge that connected man and his gods.

They catered for the building of those elaborate edifices and temples for their many gods. The Assyrian city of Nippur was built four thousand years ago by a magician for a god named Erich. Those brokers that mediated between gods and mankind have gained great power and ruled over even the most isolated tribes in the world. They used rewards like reverence and gold which increased their power further and enabled them to embark on campaigns of plundering and to overpower their neighboring peoples. These mediators have abused their power many times. They imposed terrible penalties on the few people who dared to revolt against their philosophy.

It was only a matter of time until rulers started to present themselves as gods, as did the Pharaohs of Egypt and the Caesars of ancient Rome.

Strange practices began to develop in many places across the world. Vast, spacious China was a cradle for many rituals and such rulers that enthroned themselves '*Sons of the Sky*.' Some of the rulers I have met were on the verge of insanity for example the last ruler of the Shang Dynasty. I witnessed how he burned himself to death following his defeat on the battlefield.

Human beliefs regarding the creation of the world involve a considerable amount of baseless legends and senseless exaggerations. One common belief claims that the world was created after the sons of god had slaughtered their master god and gave slices of his flesh … to that same god!

Many nations after they were defeated on the battlefield, changed their faith in one certain god to a belief in a stronger god or sometimes they were converted forcefully by the conquerors. That happened to two tribes of the ten lost ones who are currently dwelling in Afghanistan. The *Pashtunwali* tribes claim that they are the descendants of the ten lost tribes, but today they are converted to the Islamic religion.

I, the Son of the Planets, have witnessed the establishment of your world. I have seen the first steps of human beings and the evolvement of their exotic rituals not only on planet Earth but all across the Seven Worlds. I have visited many planets, and wherever I appeared … I was worshiped as a god. I was deified in many worlds as a god when funny temples and ridiculous myths were inspired by me. My image was adorned by funny stories in your world too. It will take a long time before your world will find the truth and these rituals will disappear. Planet Earth, like many other planets, adheres to so many rites and beliefs that instruct followers on the path to eternal happiness. If mankind does not defeat his inherent wickedness and totally overcome it, all his rituals and beliefs will not be of any help, and by his own stupidity, he will disappear from the face of the earth. All those brokers that mediate between man and god, with their worshiping, their bows, their holy charms, and their holy ghosts, will not help on the last day on Earth. The destruction of forests and wildlife on Earth also destroys your planet fast. If you won't stop this horrible destruction and be united, your race will disappear in the infinite space, and Earth will become desolated like the moon.

Will the human beasts destroy your tiny world? Will human wisdom overcome the pursuit of respect, control, and avarice by human beasts? All the witchcraft stories of the magicians and brokers of god, that promise human happiness and eternal life in return for practicing their rituals, are total lies. They are hopeless and they have nothing to do with the truth.

After my own world's last war we moved our planet to the Triangle of Light. However, many other planets that I visited have disappeared in the face of some apocalyptic wars and life there vanished after these wars. In conclusion, in the Seven Skies there are many still and lifeless planets. Life on them was extinct after the total chaos and power struggles of man and now they don't have any conquerors and conquered.

Then Arthur D'Acosta concluded, "I do not have much time left. I have to complete my task. Who knows, maybe we will meet again, and then I would be able to tell you more. In the meantime, be careful not to say anything to anybody. Remember that the black ring should never be removed from your finger."

Chapter 18

Conclusion or ...

Hundreds of vehicles passed on the crowded streets in the colorful city of Jerusalem. A shabby black taxi joined the winding racing line of snake-like lights that moved toward the Old City. Sue, Mr. D'Acosta, and I were sitting in the taxi very quietly. My eyes were looking out the window, but my thoughts were at the Black Mountains and at the wondrous land in the bowels of the earth. Would Mr. D'Acosta be successful in finding the holiest of all, the heart of the Jewish nation, the Tables of the Law? Are the intriguing designs on the diary really a secret map that leads to their secret place? Such were the questioned that were troubling my mind again and again. "The Old City," the driver announcement in English, interrupted my daydreaming about the ten lost tribes and their enchanted land in the bowels of the earth.

We left the taxi and entered the Old City. Pillars of smoke filled the street with zesty smells of Middle Eastern foods. A few silent and weary-looking peddlers were sitting next to their merchandise, watching the masses of people passing by them. They were not the type of peddlers who would chase you like vampires. Now, at sundown, no energy was left for them to follow potential customers or to declare loudly about their merchandise.

We silently and lightly climbed the quiet street. The three of us passed there like shadows; we were engulfed by thoughts about distant places. No one noticed our passing. A mild westerly wind made the chain of colorful lamps jitter around in their hanging places above the openings of the stores, while long shadows fidgeted in a devilish dance on the stone walls.

In each step I took, I felt the tension rising and flowing like fire in my veins. We soon left the main street, turning into a path that climbed up a mountain. Mr. D'Acosta was holding a cloth bag with the diary inside, the diary that changed my life. Every now and then he took a piece of paper out of his pocket, examines it with a tiny flashlight, and continued to walk up the mountain.

Fifteen minutes later he took out a compass, placed it on one of the pages of the diary that was full of designs, and raised his head toward the stars, mumbling a few words. He then lifted his hand toward the Big Dipper, splayed the fingers of his left hand, and, after long consideration, stepped in the direction of his thumb.

He took exactly one hundred steps, and then he stopped and started to dig in the ground with a long, sharp knife. After a while, he unearthed a large stone, kneeled, and started to sweep his hand across it very carefully. After he removed the dirt from its surface, he illuminated its right part with his flashlight. I peeked at it from over his shoulder and saw an arrow-like slit grooved deep in it. He stood up, examined his diary, the compass, and announced quietly, "I am obviously on the right track." Several people passed by, watched us with curiosity, and then moved on.

About an hour passed since we have arrived there and I felt very tired and could barely walk. D'Acosta examined the drawings in the diary again. He looked at the stars for a long time and then continued to walk. For a moment, I felt as if he was unaware of my presence. He looked like a man floating in faraway worlds. A mysterious smile was on his face. "This is it! On the left of the Mount of Olives," he whispered and kept walking slowly up the mountain.

The moon that formerly poured its light over the footpath, hid behind a cloud and deepened the darkness until it was difficult to continue further. After a few steps, I saw an isolated house surrounded by a tall stone wall. We approached it carefully.

"One hundred and eighty steps directly in the direction of the North Star," D'Acosta mumbled several times. "We have a problem! We must cross this wall! Thirty steps behind it there is an ancient well. I have been searching for this well since the day I arrived in the Old City. I am certain that I'm closer from ever to my destination," he whispered and rubbed his fingers with satisfaction.

"Mr. D'Acosta, wouldn't it be better if we come here during daylight?"

"No, this is impossible, and you will soon know why not."

After thinking for a moment, Mr. D'Acosta turned to the large gate on the wall and knocked on it several times. There was silence. He knocked again, this time forcefully. A light came on up in the house indicating that someone had been awakened. A few moments later, several heads were peeking through the windows, calling out to us in a language that we did not understand.

"We do not understand," I responded in English.

"Hada Inglizi"[12] I heard them saying to one another loudly. All the windows were closed at once as we heard the sound of footsteps stomping fast down a staircase. The iron door opened and a man dressed in a galabiya, dress-like robe, stood at the door holding a kerosene lamp.

"What sir want?" he asked in broken English, thrusting the light from his flashlight at our eyes.

"We are looking for an ancient well," Mr. D'Acosta said in perfect Arabic. I was amazed.

"Oh," the man said, surprised. "Are you Arab?"

"No, I am a Spaniard," D'Acosta answered quickly.

Soon they were engaged in a lively conversation. The door to the big yard opened with a screeching sound, and we were invited to enter his home in a most respectful manner. After being entertained in our host's hospitable home, D'Acosta stood up, thanked his host, and gave

---

[12] They are Englishmen

him a few bills. At first, the man objected to receiving the money, but his objection ceased when he saw the venomous look at his wife's eyes.

A few moments later our host went out walking ahead of us, holding a kerosene lamp to light our way. After several steps, we stood near the well. A large and heavy ring-like stone was set over the mouth of the well. After a short conversation between Mr. D'Acosta and his host, the man turned around and went back into his house.

"How did you manage to convince the man to let us see the well at this late hour?" I asked.

"Very simple. I gave him a fair amount of money. My friend, money is motivating to most people in our world. The price of conscience is low. At first, our host refused to receive any payment, but I knew that it was a game of prestige and he was attracted to my money as a moth is attracted to a flame."

"How did you explain that we wanted to get into his yard in the middle of the night?"

"I told him that I am doing research in archaeology and that I am especially looking for ancient wells. When he asked why I am doing it at night rather than during the day, I told him that the hot sun is damaging to my delicate skin. I have no idea whether this explanation was convincing, but it makes no difference. With my money, I easily achieved my goal. Truly enough I heard him whispering to his wife. Both of them agreed that I am insane, but, my friend, money amounts to more than any insanity."

"But why are you interested in seeing this well at this late hour of the night? Why shouldn't we visit this place during morning hours?"

"Ha, ha, ha," he chuckled. This was the first time that I had heard him laugh. "Would you like to be accompanied by all the town dignitaries? Any move that I have made in this town has attracted dozens of prying eyes. How could I possibly enter the well while all the members of the house follow each of my steps? I don't need their nosy looks."

"Enter the well?!" I marveled.

"Shhh," he whispered to me. "Do not raise your voice. The walls have ears."

"How are we going to remove this weighty stone from its place?"

"Dear Dan, what happened to your patience? Wait and you will soon see how I am going into the well. My dear friends, the moment to say goodbye has arrived. In a few minutes, I will be on my way into the network of tunnels that lead to a place underneath the Temple Mount, to the place where the Jewish temple stood before its destruction by the Romans.

"At this moment we are at the opening to the network of tunnels that were quarried by the Jews, during the siege of Jerusalem by the Romans. When the high priests saw that the holy vessels were in danger, they rushed to prepare imitations and placed them instead of the original ones. Then they quickly dug a network of tunnels and concealed the real vessels there. Later on, they sealed the entrances to the tunnels except for this secret one here, at this well"

"What is the connection between the diary and this place?" I asked, subduing my eagerness to know.

"As you know, the Sons of Israel had undermined the words of the scribe Zvi Ben Yosef, who told them that he had met the Son of the Planets and that this visitor had revealed to him the hiding place of the holy vessels and of the Tables of the Law. After many years in the land of the ten lost tribes, I learned that they knew nothing of the diary, which was buried with the scribe. I carefully studied the mysterious designs in the diary. For many long days, I sat down and researched the diary, in conjunction with the precious material I found in the books at the big library. Eventually, I realized that I could find the secret hiding place of the holy vessels of the Temple. This discovery really shocked me, while my excitement overcame me and left my spirit restless. The understanding that the designs in the diary are decipherable secret codes that might lead me to the sacred treasures inspired me with celestial happiness. Due to this code, I will be able to proceed and discover some further codes that would lead me to the holy vessels. It is obvious that after thousands of years the terrain had been totally changed making it impossible to track using the ciphered signs. This is the reason why I wandered around for many hours trying to find the signs that lead to the well".

"A short time before we met on Masada, I managed to cipher another segment of the map in the diary. It was the stone with the mark of the arrow I showed you. I have searched for this sign for a long time. Now you can understand that one should not give up. Despite the many hardships, I did not give up on my sacred goal. Now, my friends, I feel the nearest I have ever been to my much-coveted goal — the treasures of the Temple and the Tables of the Law."

"Aren't you concerned that the professor might find out, the meaning of the designs and will follow your footsteps?"

"No, I am not at all concerned," he said and smiled. "Within a few days, this treasure is going to be in my hands." As he was saying these words, he pulled a flashlight, threw some light on the stone lid uttering in Hebrew, "Goodbye and see you again."

And Before I could respond with 'Goodbye', he sank through the stone lid. I stood amazed for a moment at this extraordinary sight. *How is it possible to enter a stone? Did it truly happen? Am I dreaming?* I pinched myself to see if I was dreaming. I looked at Sue and caught a wondering look in her eyes. For some time, we just stood there petrified and immersed in excitement.

I do not remember how we made our way back to the hotel, but after we arrived we sat for many hours staring into space, pondering, whether was it all just a dream? Would we meet our friend D'Acosta again? Would he eventually find the treasures of the Temple and the Tables of the Law?

The following day our journey in the Holy Land would end and we'd return to school. Our minds were still impressed by those endless tunnels that encircle our planet, which lead to the subterranean Land, the hiding place of the ten lost tribes, the most persecuted people in the world, who found there a safe haven from the cruelty of the human beast.

✡   ✡   ✡

The first rays of dawn found the three of us in hectic preparation for our return home. At exactly 08:00 a.m. Sue and I were down at the taxi helping Dad with our baggage and soon we were off, heading out of that most wonderful city. Dad had returned from his work in Rehovot late the prior evening. He had no clue of the adventures Sue and I experienced in his absence. With the black rings on our fingers, we weren't even able to tell him.

It took us precisely one hour to arrive at the airport, where we had to wait until 10:00 a.m. when our departing flight was due to board. We three sat in the concourse café having the coffee and eclairs that Dad had bought, watching the throng of people walking by. And then, out of nowhere, we noticed Mr. D'Acosta greeting a good-looking girl who was just coming out through the arrival lounge exit. He took her by the hand and quickly they both left the airport. Sue pressed my hand. "What's going on here?" she whispered.

"I have many questions but we must stop for now. Remember, the walls have ears." I replied with a whisper.

Soon we heard our flight number being called and we headed for the departure gate. Once we were on board, I settled into my seat and leaned back. I was unable to fall asleep and after a while the airplane took off and sped upward, leaving the airport a shrinking sight below us, and rising on its course up toward the clouds. For several long minutes I sat captivated by the sight of the age-old country below us, still with many questions in mind: *Did Mr. D'Acosta find the treasures of the Temple? Where is he headed to now? Who was the girl that he took by the hand?*

THE END

or is it?

About the Author

Yossi Soika

I was born a year after the end of World War II when my parents made their way from Russia to an immigrant camp in Germany. Two and a half years later their way led them back to our fatherland, Israel. From the age of four, I carry with me the first memories of the neighborhood of small huts in Afula. That desolated hut neighborhood amidst the fields nourished me with the entire materials for the dreams that attend me to this day.

Today I'm the father of two sons and a daughter, but the sweetest of all are my eight grandchildren … the prospect of a wonderful future. For the last ten years, I have lived with my partner Nava, who excels in many ways and to whom I dedicate this book.

My mother, at the age of 93 is energetic and active to this day and calls me "my child." What else can I say about it? Mothers know everything.

And still, I'm immersed in childhood dreams …